Charlie

and Me

421 MILES FROM HOME

MARK LOWERY

 YELLOW JACKET

This is a work of fiction. Any references to historical events, real people, or real places are used fictitiously. Other names, characters, places, and events are products of the author's imagination, and any resemblance to actual events or places or persons, living or dead, is entirely coincidental.

🐝 YELLOW JACKET

An imprint of Bonnier Publishing USA
251 Park Avenue South, New York, NY 10010
Copyright © 2018 by Mark Lowery
All rights reserved, including the right of reproduction in whole or in part in any form.
Yellow Jacket Books is a trademark of Bonnier Publishing USA, and associated colophon is a trademark of Bonnier Publishing USA.
Manufactured in the United States of America   BVG 0718
First Edition
10 9 8 7 6 5 4 3 2 1
Library of Congress Cataloging-in-Publication Data is available upon request.
ISBN 978-1-4998-0756-1
yellowjacketreads.com
bonnierpublishingusa.com

For my family

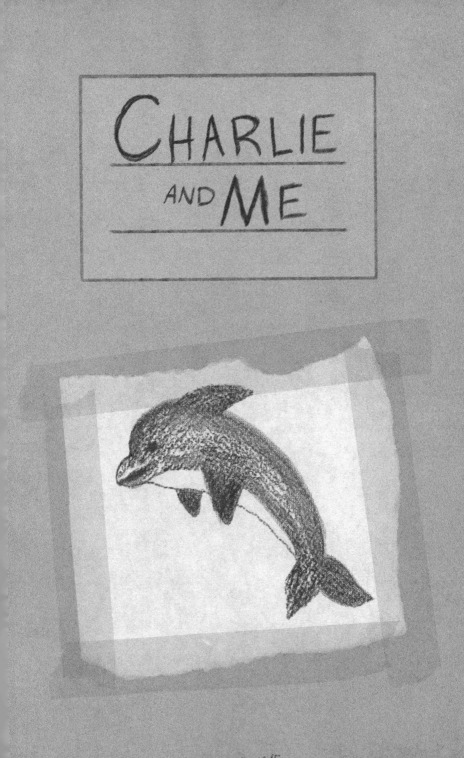

CHARLIE
AND ME

PROPERTY OF MARTIN TOMPKINS

Leaping Dolphin

Your life is a leaping dolphin
Bursting out from
Blackness,
Blankness
Into brilliant sunshine.
Twisting,
Flipping,
Straining
In whatever direction
You choose.
And scattering
Infinity and one
Tiny droplets of water,
Each one briefly containing
A tiny, distorted reflection
Of yourself.
You are a leaping dolphin.
A glorious example
Of what it means
To be alive.

By Martin Tompkins
Age 13

Stage 1

886 Plungington Road to Preston Station
via Farook's Supernews

Distance—1.5 miles
Walking

Cookies and Belly Buttons

My little brother Charlie's sitting cross-legged on the floor of the corner shop, humming with his eyes closed. He does this kind of thing a lot.

"Hurry up," I say, giving him a friendly kick with my raggedy old Reebok. "We've got a train to catch."

Charlie wipes his nose on his sleeve. "Give me a minute, Marty," he replies. "I'm just charging up the laser in my belly button."

He *says* this kind of thing a lot too.

My brother, Charlie, doesn't have a laser in his belly button. I know this for a fact. Not that I've ever *studied* it. But if you share a small bedroom with your brother for ten years, then you end up pretty well acquainted with his whole body whether you like it or not.

Charlie isn't like ordinary kids. He is one in a million. In fact, he's one in a *Charlillion*. A Charlillion, by the way, is a number he invented that is one more than infinity. I tried to explain to him that you can't have one more than infinity. Infinity means it goes on forever. Charlie called me a banana-brain. He can be very childish when he wants to be.

At poetry club in school, Mr. Hendrix sometimes plays a game to warm us up. You've got to talk about a topic for thirty seconds without stopping or repeating yourself. Here's what I'd say about Charlie:

"Lazy eye, massive head, snores like a hippo, often ill, weird taste in food, terrible memory, always out of breath because of his asthma, skinny, cheeky, can't do anything for himself or concentrate for more than two seconds, brain's inside out, no understanding of danger. My absolute best friend in the whole entire world."

I'd have to stop there. You could talk about Charlie for a Charlillion seconds if you wanted to, and you'd never run out of things to say.

"Which cookies do you want?" I ask him. Mr. Farook is watching us carefully from behind the counter. Each time I glance over he's there, leaning right back so he can see along the aisle. I smile at him, but his face stays blank. I'm starting to feel queasy.

Charlie pushes his milk-bottle glasses up on his nose and squints at me through his lazy eye. His good eye has a Peppa Pig patch on it so that his lazy one learns to work harder. *Peppa Pig* is one of Charlie's favorite shows, despite him being at least six years older than the average viewer. "Why can't we have one of the cookies from your backpack?"

I clutch my backpack to my chest, squeezing the hard corners of the *special-leftover-from-Christmas* cookie tin that I took from home. Of course Charlie saw me steal the cookies. He sees everything, even though his eyes are terrible. Maybe he doesn't have a laser in his belly button. Maybe it's a security camera.

"They're special," I say. "They're for when we get there."

"Get where?"

"Where we're going."

I don't want to tell him where we're going until we're on the train. He'll only get excited. And trust me, an excited Charlie is not what I need in my life at quarter to seven on a Saturday morning. Imagine filling a puppy with blue Smarties and Lemon Fanta, then bouncing it up and down on a trampoline; that's Charlie when he's excited.

"Are there any of those chocolate wheel cookies in the tin?" he asks.

"They're called Wagon Wheels, Charlie. Of course I have them," I say.

"What about the ones with all the jam in the middle? They're my favorite. Eighty percent cookie. Fifteen percent jam."

"What's the other five percent?" I ask, just because he's always got a weird answer.

Charlie sniffs hard. "Dreams."

Told you. Brain inside out. I shake my head.

He settles on a pack of the cookies filled with jam and dreams, or as they're known to the rest of us, Jammie Dodgers (an excellent choice), and we go to pay.

When I get my wallet out, I accidentally flash my wad of twenty-pound* notes at Mr. Farook, which is a mistake. His big, furry eyebrows shoot up on his

---

*At the time of this printing, 1 pound is the equivalent of 1.33 US dollars.

forehead. The guy's like a bloodhound for money. The police should use him to sniff out where criminals hide their cash.

"Going somewhere special?" he says, nodding at my backpack.

I'm trying to figure out how to answer this when Charlie butts in.

"Switzerland," he says seriously. "I'm getting my belly-button laser upgraded."

By the time Mr. Farook can reply, we're out on the street.

"Nice work, boss," I say, giving Charlie a fist bump. He flashes me his cheekiest, squintiest, one-eyed grin and we set off walking to the train station.

Walrus-Flopping

There's one thing everyone needs to know about Charlie: He is a miracle.

He was born early—about fifteen weeks before he was supposed to. Mum and Dad never let me visit him when he was in the hospital because I was only three, but I've seen a photo: a minuscule, scrawny red alien in a fish tank with a woolly hat on and Ping-Pong-ball eyelids. There are tubes sprouting out of his mouth and wires attached to his chest and machines blinking all around him. Dad's finger is in the corner of the shot, and it's almost as long as Charlie's whole body.

They kept him in the hospital for three months because he was so sick. A machine had to breathe for him because his lungs were a pair of useless wet sponges. His heart kept breaking down, so he had to have four emergency operations on it. And, after all that, he caught a really serious infection from one of his breathing tubes. A couple of times the doctors told Mum and Dad to go in and say goodbye because *this could be* "the Night."

It makes me feel sick when I think how close he came to . . . you know . . .

But somehow, he fought and fought and stayed alive. He was even in the newspaper because the doctors thought it was so incredible. We've still got the clippings in a frame on the mantelpiece: "Meet Charlie the Miracle Baby," "Fighting Fit Charlie Back from the Dead," "Alive and Kicking."

The day he finally came home is one of my earliest memories. I can picture Dad holding me on one knee with Charlie in the crook of his other arm. "Meet your baby brother, big guy," he said, black rings around his eyes and his voice catching in his throat. "You're gonna have to look after him."

So I guess I always have: holding his hand to cross the road, cutting up his food, tying his shoelaces for him because he's so clumsy, making sure his bag's packed in the morning because he always forgets everything, biting the bruises out of his apples because he's got a weird thing about them, teaching him to throw and catch because he's terrible at it, and even sitting with him through all of his millions of appointments and checkups at the hospital.

A few years ago, Mum told me I was the best big brother in the world. It was cool of her to say so, but I don't see it like that. Charlie's a laugh, but he can be like a lost kitten sometimes—bumbling through life all confused and unaware of what's going on around him. It's not like I'm a good person or anything. I just *have* to help him out.

Still, Charlie doesn't always like me to help him. He likes to do things his own way. Mum says he's a free spirit, but I call him a loon. In the nicest possible way, of course.

Even when he was a baby he was like that. It took him ages to learn to walk, but he never let it hold him back. He used to do this strange lopsided crawl—the walrus flop, Dad called it—which was surprisingly fast. One time, when he was nearly two, Mum put him in his playpen (aka "the Cage" because it was the only way to keep him still) and went upstairs to do something.

When she came back down ten minutes later, he'd disappeared. The front door was open. She thought he'd been snatched, and she ran outside in a blind panic. And there he was, walrus-flopping across the road, cars slamming on their brakes and swerving out of the way.

When trying to piece together what'd happened afterward, Mum thought that he'd been so bored that he'd bitten his way through the seam of the plastic mesh wall of the playpen. Then he'd yanked the wall back to make an escape hole, crawled across the living room, somehow opened the front door, and made a break for it.

Then there was the day when he was four and he decided he didn't like his eyebrows. He said they were freaking him out. So, being Charlie, he shaved them clean off with Dad's razor. There was blood everywhere. He looked like he'd been attacked with a potato peeler.

And how about when he played the Innkeeper in the school nativity? We still watch the DVD every Christmas. He only had one line to remember: "Sorry. No room at the inn." But this is Charlie we're talking about.

After telling Mary and Joseph that they could stay in the Honeymoon Suite (who knows where he got that from) and that the donkey could have its own room, he pulled the baby Jesus out from under Mary's dress, held Him up by His ankle and announced: "Behold! The King of the shoes!" On the DVD you can almost hear the teacher slapping her forehead offscreen when she says, "It's King of the *Jews*. And put Him back; you're a day early."

Invisible Boys

After leaving Farook's, we walk quickly along Plungington Road toward the station. It's still insanely early, so the late-September air is cool and there aren't many people about—a few shopkeepers and café owners pulling up their shutters and setting up signs outside their shops, a couple of students staggering home from the night before.

I try not to look at any of them. I'm expecting someone to stop us and ask us what we're doing out at this time, or ask us if our parents know where we are, or call the police. But no one seems to notice us. They've all got their own lives to think about. We're invisible.

This is a good thing. We need to get to the train station and onto a train without Mum and Dad realizing we're gone. If they find out what I'm doing, they'll go ballistic. They're so protective of Charlie it's unbelievable. He's not even allowed out on his scooter without an armed guard and a full set of injections.

As we walk, I start to relax a bit. Every step gets us closer to safety. Once we've got our tickets, we'll be on our way. Break things down into little bits and they don't seem so scary anymore.

"Jammie Dodger?" says Charlie, offering me the pack.

I take one, and we clink them in midair. "Breakfast of champions," I say.

For a short while, we walk alongside each other, munching on our cookies and not saying anything. It's rare to have silence when Charlie's around, and it doesn't last long.

"You still haven't told me where we're going," he says. He's found a stick, and he's dragging it along some railings outside a church.

"Somewhere good, I promise," I say, but it's still too soon to let him know. I need to change the subject. "How about I test you on your times tables?"

I always try to help him with his homework. He struggles at school because he can't focus on anything

16

and he's a bit hyperactive. Mum says this is common with kids who were born early. She's always having fights with the teachers about it because he can't be expected to learn like everyone else, can he? And if they let him use his imagination instead of trying to stuff his poor little head full of useless information, then maybe he'd have a chance in life.

She's very sensitive when it comes to Charlie. And she's sort of right—everyone thinks he's dumb, but in some ways he's mega smart. His brain's just wired up differently, that's all.

Even so, the teachers *have* got a point. When he was in second grade, he got a letter home saying, "Charlie did not complete today's spelling test because he was pretending to be a tortoise." Dad thought this was hilarious and stuck it on the fridge.

"Times tables? On a Saturday?" says Charlie, flinging the stick down. The baggy sleeves of his sweater swing around afterward. "Child cruelty! I'm calling the RSPCA."

"What?" I say. "The *animal* charity?"

"Yeah," replies Charlie as though this is what he

meant all along. "I'll tell 'em you keep a . . . a pig in a shoe box and . . . you throw darts at it and you make it smoke cigarettes. They'll lock you up, and then I'll be safe."

I scoff. "Come on. Which times table are you learning at the moment?"

"The one times table," he says immediately. "One times one is one. Two times one is t—"

"Yeah right!" I interrupt, giving him a friendly jab in the arm. "Nobody learns the ones. Let's do the eights. One times eight is eight. Two times eight is . . . ?"

Charlie looks off into the distance and scratches his head. "Er . . . fourteen . . ."

"Try again."

"Twelve . . . no seventeen."

"It can't be seventeen," I sigh. I try to be patient with him, but I'm pretty good at math and working with Charlie can get *seriously* frustrating. "We've been through this. Seventeen's not in any of the times tables. It's a prime number."

This was a mistake. Immediately he's talking about something else.

"Prime number? Is that like a prime minister?" he says, and before I can answer, he's off. "If I was a prime minister, I'd make everyone wear top hats."

We reach a crosswalk, and I push the button. "What? Why?" I say, my brain struggling to catch up.

"I like 'em. Plus then I'd be taller than everyone."

"But they'd all be wearing top hats too."

He thinks for a second. "Yeah. But only the *prime minister* would be allowed to wear high heels."

"In-*credible*," I say, puffing out my cheeks and pressing the button again. Without warning, Charlie just steps out into the road even though the orange hand is still showing. I drag him back right before a car roars past. Luckily I'm always expecting him to do things like this. "Careful!"

No understanding of danger whatsoever.

"Hey, Marty," he says, switching the conversation again like nothing just happened. "Why did we have to leave without telling Mum and Dad?"

I bite my lip. I knew he'd ask sooner or later, so I'd already prepared my answer. "I didn't want to wake them. Dad didn't get in from work until after midnight."

He scrunches up his face. "Are you sure we're allowed out this early?"

"Yep. It's fine. Anyway, I'll text them when we're on the train."

"How will you do that?" he sniffs.

"My phone, of course."

"But I saw you hide your phone in your sock drawer when I was getting dressed."

I say nothing, focusing hard on my finger as it jabs the button again and again. I told you. He sees *everything*. CCTV in his belly button. And probably satellite dishes on his nipples.

"Why *would* you do that, Marty?" he continues. "It's like you don't want anyone to be able to get ahold of us. And if you *are* going to hide something, you really should *close* the drawer afterward, you know."

The walking signal flashes, and I pull Charlie across the road. "Have another Jammie Dodger," I mutter. I need to keep calm and positive, so for the rest of the journey into town, I try to think up a poem in my head.

You Only Live Once

A Haiku

You only live once
So you might as well just eat
Cookies for breakfast.

By Martin Tompkins
Age 13

Stage 2

Preston Railway Station Ticket Office
to the Bathrooms on Platform Three
and Back Again

Distance—820 feet (approx.)
Walking

The Station

I'm not happy about how busy the station is: three young soldiers pretending not to struggle with their massive duffel bags; a homeless guy sitting on the floor between the ticket windows, head down between his knees and cap by his feet; two confused foreign students squinting at the departure screen; a cluster of Preston North End fans off to an away game, some of them chugging cans of cider even though it's only seven o'clock in the morning; and, worst of all, two police officers watching them carefully from sixty feet away.

In the line for the ticket window, I take my notebook out of my bag, but I can't find the piece of paper I tucked in there with all the train times on it. I check again, then double-check inside my backpack. For a moment, I think I've seen it. There's a loose bit of paper, but when I pull it out, I'm disappointed. It's just this mileage chart thing I printed off that tells you how much distance there is between all the towns. Whenever we're going on a long journey, I like to know how far we've traveled and how far's left to go. Like I said, everything seems easier when you break it down into little pieces. Even so, it's not going to help me know which train to catch.

Great start.

I put my notebook and the mileage chart away again and notice my hands are shaking. All the people and the police are making me nervous.

Keep calm. Look normal.

I reach the window and smile at the woman behind the counter. Her badge says "Sue—Trainee." Big, brown hair. Pink lipstick. Round face. Charlie's off to the side. He's found a timetable-holder that spins and he's whizzing it around and around.

What am I supposed to do now? Sue leans forward and nods as if to say, "Get on with it." With a deep breath, I speak into the microphone. "Hi, Sue," I say. *Am I meant to use her name?* "We'd . . . er . . . like to go to St. Bernards."

The microphone amplifies my voice, like it's

trying to announce where we're going to the police behind me. The last thing I need is *them* sniffing around asking me questions.

Sue's painted-on eyebrows rise up her forehead. "As in St. Bernards in *Cornwall*?"

She says *Cornwall* like it's somewhere near Jupiter.

I'm about to say yes when Charlie looks over. "ST. BERNARDS?!" he cries. "No way! Oh wow!"

Before I can stop him, his sweater's up over his face and he's running around the station like he's just scored a goal at Wembley Stadium.

I told you he'd get excited.

"Don't worry about my brother. He's got an inside-out brain," I say to Sue, rubbing my neck and trying not to look agitated.

She looks at me like *I'm* the weird one. "You *do* know how far that is . . . ?"

I peep over my shoulder. Charlie is looping around the foreign students, arms out like an airplane. They're too busy to have noticed him yet, which *would* be funny except for the fact that sooner or later someone *will* notice him. I was hoping we could keep this low-key.

"Three hundred and seventy miles," I reply, turning back to Sue and doing my best to remain calm and level. "I checked on my mileage chart. We went there on vacation last year with our mum and dad. Charlie chose it because he liked the name; he said it sounds like one of those dogs. You know the massive ones they use in the mountains to rescue people. But it turns out it's a lovely place. They've got a lighthouse. Have you ever been?"

I'm talking too much. *Shut up. Shut up.*

Sue taps away at her computer. "No, sadly not. . . . Single or return?" she says. There's a hint of bored frustration in her voice.

"Oh," I say. My palms are sweaty. I practiced this conversation over and over in front of the mirror so I'd sound natural, but this isn't a question I'd been expecting. I push my knuckle into my eye to try to ease the throbbing pain that's building up. This isn't going to plan. "I'm . . . er . . . not sure."

As soon as the words come out of my mouth, I realize exactly what she meant. Simple question: "Are you coming back or not?" I feel like a complete idiot. Sue nods toward the people behind me. "Well, I've got a line, so . . ."

Even though I know the answer to the question now, I shuffle to the side, head down like a slapped dog. An older woman steps up to the window and starts jabbering away about quiet coaches and super-saver advances and aisle seats. There's a whole language for buying train tickets that I've never heard of. How do people know all this stuff? Why don't they teach us it in school? All we learn is triangles and books and swimming and . . . *why am I thinking about swimming?*

My whole body feels shaky, like I'm standing on top of a rickety fence in the wind. I'm taking deep breaths and trying to calm myself, and it's made worse because Charlie's back at my shoulder going on and on and on about how St. Bernards is the best place in the world and how he can't believe we're going back there. His questions are endless. Will we go to the beach? Will I buy him fish and chips? Do you think we'll see the dolphin? And I can feel one of my headaches coming on because we're not even out of the station and it's all starting to go wrong, and my hands are over my ears and my eyes are clamped shut and the lights are flashing in my head.

I feel a hand on my shoulder. It makes me jump, and when I turn around, a policewoman's standing there asking me if I'm all right. I swallow down the huge egg in my throat and splutter: "Just a headache. Need to splash some water on my face."

And I manage to hold it together long enough to grab Charlie and stumble down the ramp to the bathroom on platform three.

St. Bernards

Of course I knew Charlie would get excited. It's not his fault. I mean, he's the whole reason for us going to St. Bernards in the first place.

We went there on vacation last summer and it was amazing. That was fourteen months ago—when we still did things as a family. Back before things got a bit crummy at home. Back before Dad started working a Charlillion hours a week and Mum started sleeping in.

It was a Friday night, and summer break had officially begun. Mum was preparing for vacation by cleaning the whole house. Dad joked she was making it clean for the burglars. I'd just finished helping Charlie pack his bag (*No*, I had to tell him, *you can't put an open carton of yogurt in there. I don't care if Big Ted gets hungry. . . .*) when Dad called us together on the sofa. He said now that we were getting older, we might not have many more family vacations so we should make it a good one. A proper adventure. After all, it'd taken him two years to save up for it so being miserable was not an option.

Charlie saluted with his tongue sticking out. "Yes, sir!" he barked.

Dad grinned and ruffled Charlie's hair.

We set off at 10:30 that night to miss the traffic. All four of us crammed into our little Fiesta with the roof rack on and "School's Out" blaring from the stereo. The back end of the car was so weighed down it was practically dragging along the road. Charlie was bouncing around in his booster seat like a flea with an itchy backside. I'd never seen him so full of it. Munching sweets. Singing. Telling jokes. Me, I guess I prefer to sit back a bit and let him shine. I had a road atlas on my knees and I slowly followed the M6 south with my finger, checking off the junctions as we passed them and flicking back to the mileage chart at the front to see how far there was until the next big town.

At around 2:00 a.m. we pulled up at the rest stop to sleep in the car. It was just like Dad said, a proper adventure. Well, for a couple of hours, anyway. Until some security guard knocked on the car window and told us to cough up twenty pounds or get lost.

We got lost, with Charlie mooning out of the rear window. Dad said he was awake now, so he might as well drive straight through. He's used to night shifts driving the forklift, so it didn't bother him. The rest of us slept on and off, and we arrived red-eyed in St. Bernards at 7:30 in the morning. Our RV wasn't going to be ready until the afternoon, so Dad parked the car and wandered off to find some breakfast.

The town was just waking up: the smell of fresh bread from bakeries, shopkeepers dragging racks of flip-flops and beach balls out of shops called Wild Bill's Surf Shack or Bob's Budget Beach Hut, street cleaners emptying trash cans and aiming half-hearted kicks at the cocky seagulls that scrounged around the cobblestones.

We'd been wandering around for a few minutes before we caught a glimpse of the ocean, a narrow strip of blue squeezed between two cottages. "Might as well have a peek," Dad said. We followed a steep lane until it opened out onto the seafront and WOW!

It was incredible.

The town nestled above a bay, about a quarter of a mile wide. It was a perfect semicircle, like the sea had taken a great big bite out of the land. Colorful cottages seemed to tumble topsy-turvy down the slope toward it. The tide was in, and fishing boats bobbed up and down on a sparkling sheet of turquoise. To our right, the bay was fringed by jagged rocks that concealed the rest of the coast. At the far side, over to the left, an old stone jetty stretched out to sea, with a small, white lighthouse perched at the end of it.

Dad whistled.

Mum squeezed his hand and said, "Beautiful."

"What are they looking at?" said Charlie, squinting at a huddle of people on the other side of the road. There were about seven of them standing along the railings and pointing out to sea.

Charlie didn't wait for an answer from us. He darted across the road, right in front of a car that screeched to a halt just in time. The rest of us chased after him. Mum grabbed him by the arm. "Don't you ever do that again! I couldn't bear—"

But Charlie wasn't listening. "Wow!" he said, pointing over Mum's shoulder. "Look at *that!*"

"What?" said Mum, her fingers instinctively relaxing as she turned to look.

Charlie wriggled out of her grasp, peeled off his eye patch, and pressed himself up against the railings. "*That!* Behind that big, blue boat. Next to the dinghy."

Poetry

I've been sitting on the lid of the toilet for five minutes, just breathing in and out with my head pressed against the cold, metal wall. This eventually calms me down, in spite of the horrible smell in here.

Things got a bit wobbly at the ticket office, but I managed to avoid a total disaster and everything's okay now.

Except it's not.

Not really. I've sneaked out of my house and I've kidnapped my brother, and now we're running away to the far end of the country for the weekend. If—sorry, when—Mum and Dad find out, they'll murder me. That's if the police at the station don't arrest me first.

I rub my face and sit up straight. *Pull yourself together*. We've made it here, so we've successfully accomplished stage one. The hardest part is the next bit: buying the tickets and getting on the train. Once we do that, we're on our way.

I pull the notebook with the picture of a dolphin on the front out of my backpack. The book's almost finished—maybe eight more pages—so it takes a while to flick through to a blank page. I fold back the cover and jot down the poem I'd been thinking of on the way into town. A haiku. Five syllables. Seven syllables. Five syllables. Just like Mr. Hendrix taught me in poetry club. There's something neat and symmetrical about it that reassures me that everything's all right. The poem itself is a stupid one about cookies. Not one of my best. But writing it down and concentrating on the tip of my pen as it moves across the page makes my worries melt away.

There's a knock on the stall door. Charlie. "Have you fallen in?"

I slip the notebook back into the backpack and open the door. I could hear him messing around with the hand dryers the whole time I've been in here. He loves a good bathroom.

"Word up, brother," I say, feeling a lot more chipper now.

We stride back up the ramp to the ticket window. Making up poems always helps me figure things out, even though it's not like I'm great at it. Mr. Hendrix says it's the best way to get stuff out of your brain. He says that when he's stressed, he writes poems standing on his head. I don't think he'd like doing that in a filthy railway station bathroom.

"Decided yet?" says Sue. She's trying to look indulgent, like she cares, but I can tell she's bored stiff. The homeless guy by the window gives me a thumbs-up and a toothless smile, like he wants me to succeed. Maybe he knows we're running away and understands. This gives me a little confidence boost, and I nod back at him.

"Two child tickets to St. Bernards, coming back tomorrow," I say to Sue in my most impressive voice. On the way back up the ramp, I'd noticed that the police had followed the football fans down to a platform. The station feels a lot more comfortable without them around.

"This is so awesome!" says Charlie, leaning back against the wall next to the window, his arms spread out like a star.

"Two *children?*" Sue squawks. "You mean you're traveling all the way to St. Bernards without an adult?"

"I'm fifteen," I lie. "Mum said it was okay for us to go as long as we're back tomorrow."

Sue frowns. "I'm not sure about this. It's a really long way. I've only worked here a week. Maybe I need to speak to my manager."

"No!" I exclaim, surprised by how loud my voice is.

Sue moves her head back from the speaker. The homeless guy and the customer at the next window glance over at me.

"Actually, I forgot. I'm an adult. One *adult* round-trip ticket to St. Bernards coming back tomorrow," I say, firmly but more quietly. I'm breathing so hard my breath crackles on the microphone. In. Out. *Calm.*

Sue and Charlie both speak at the same time.

"I thought you were a child?"

"*One* adult? You can't leave me here."

"Shut up!" I hiss.

"Pardon?" says Sue sharply.

I realize that Charlie's hidden from her view because of where he's standing.

"I was talking to my brother," I explain, trying to smile.

"Hmm . . ." says Sue.

I press my forehead against the cool glass. Got to keep things under wraps this time. *Think, think.* "I'm sixteen. I just had a birthday."

"What? This exact minute?"

"Yep. I was born at eight minutes past seven, so technically I just turned sixteen. Whoops. Silly me. Wish I'd got here ten minutes ago." I force a laugh.

I'm rambling again.

Sue frowns at me. "What about your brother?"

"Yeah, what about me?" pipes up Charlie.

"He can stay here."

Sue shrugs as she taps her keyboard.

"That's not fair!" cries Charlie, so I shush him.

"That'll be a hundred and seventy-seven pounds

and thirty pence," says Sue. Is it me or is her smile a bit cruel?

I feel my knees wobble. "Really?" I squeak, gulping back the urge to cry. That'll leave me with less than ten pounds. Why didn't I check the price online? I feel like such an amateur.

"Yes. Really," says Sue, getting fed up now. "If you want to travel, you've got to pay."

I count out a stack of twenties and some coins, and drop them into the drawer. Sue pulls the lever toward her, then makes a massive deal out of checking every single penny before she shoves my tickets and my change back at me. It's like a really horrible magic trick—*marvel as I turn your life savings into a couple of orange-and-green bits of card and a few pathetic coins.*

"You'd better get a move on," says Sue. "You'll be wanting the Birmingham train. Leaves platform four in two minutes."

Moving

You think that resting
Is peaceful.
But
When you stay still
Thoughts swarm
Around your head
Like a plague of wasps
Trapped in a jam jar.
Each one stinging
Your brain in a desperate
Attempt to be noticed.
But
When you move,
You rock them to sleep.
Cute and harmless
Like a million tiny babies.

By Martin Tompkins
Age 13

Stage 3a

Preston Station to Wolverhampton Station

Distance—97 miles
Train

Near Miss

I turn and jog away from the window. I'm trying to put the tickets into my wallet as I go, but Charlie's refusing to budge. "Why didn't you get *me* a ticket, Marty? Why do I have to stay behind?"

"You don't!" I say, going back and putting my arm around his shoulder. "It's better this way. The woman at the counter was going to blow our cover. And anyway, I couldn't have afforded it."

He's still dragging his feet. "But I can't get on a train without a ticket."

"*You'll have to,*" I hiss. "If the conductor comes along, just hide, okay?"

Charlie's a master at hiding, as long as he doesn't have to stay still for too long. One time we played hide-and-seek and I couldn't find him for ages. It turned out he was trapped in the cabinet under the bathroom sink. I only realized when I heard him having an asthma attack. Dad had to free him with a hacksaw and a screwdriver.

"Now come on!" I say, and finally he starts moving. We run down the ramp to the platform, but when we get there, the train hasn't actually arrived yet. The North End fans are waiting nearby, already singing, with the police still watching on.

Charlie has a blast of his inhaler. Now that I know I don't have the paper with the train times on it, I can't help but think I've forgotten other stuff too. At least I made sure Charlie had his inhaler before he left the house; he's always getting wheezy, and he needs it with him constantly. Even so, if Mum was here I'd still get an earful for making him breathless.

I stay out of sight of the police behind a large rail map, but Charlie dodges away from me to the edge of the platform. He's leaning right out, peering into the distance. "It's coming! It's coming!"

I stomp over and pull him away from the edge. "Don't do that!" I say sternly. "Stay on this side of the yellow line."

"Sorry, Mum," Charlie tisks as we move back a couple of steps.

I notice that his shoelaces are untied, so I bend down to fix them. I always tell him to choose Velcro shoes, but he prefers laces even though he's forever tripping over them and I'm usually the one who has to tie them for him.

While I'm down there, there's a gust of air and a squeak of wheels from behind me as the train snakes into the station. Charlie suddenly bursts toward the moving carriages. "Gotta get on first!"

Before I can do anything, he's stumbled over me and we're both falling in slow motion, landing flat on the ground in a tangled heap inches from the edge of the platform. My heart's hammering. From down here I can see the huge wheels grinding slowly along the tracks like giant pizza slicers.

I haul myself up then help him roughly to his feet. "Are you trying to kill us?"

Charlie picks up his glasses, which had skittered off across the platform, and angrily puts them back on like

I've done something wrong. "I was trying to make sure we got a seat."

I shake my head. The kid is utterly nuts. What kind of person tries to get onto a moving train? Even though I'm used to his crazy behavior, my stomach is somewhere near my throat at the thought of what could've just happened. The policewoman who asked if I was okay before is looking over at us, concerned.

"Let's just get on," I huff, pulling Charlie toward the nearest open door.

We Love You, North End

"We're off!" says Charlie as the train pulls out of the station. "This is exciting! I feel like a monkey with a drum kit."

It's taken less than five minutes for him to forget that he almost got us crushed by a train. We're edging along the aisle of the swaying carriage, struggling to stay upright as we try to find somewhere to sit. At the far end of the carriage, we reach a couple of unreserved seats and plop ourselves down. Charlie's by the window, and I'm next to him, the backpack with the cookies in it safely on my lap.

The seats face backward and I smile as I watch the city disappear. Within a minute or two, we're over the river, then charging through open countryside. The train is sleek and fast, and it tilts into the bends like nothing could slow it down. Next to me, Charlie's got his face pressed against the glass.

Despite the near miss on the platform, or maybe because of it, I'm extremely happy and relieved to be on the move too. In fact, Mr. Hendrix would probably say I was feeling euphoric right now.

Thinking of Mr. Hendrix makes me remember a poem I wrote in poetry club the other day, which was all about how moving can be good for you. He said it was my best one yet; in fact, he said I'd "turned a corner" with my poetry. He asked me loads of questions, then called Mum to tell her all about it. I like Mr. Hendrix, but I wasn't exactly happy about this. Mum doesn't know I even go to poetry club; it's my secret. That evening, she tried to quiz me about the poem like mums do, but I could tell her heart wasn't really in it. I just grunted a few times and eventually she left me alone and went back to bed. It was four in the afternoon.

I ruffle Charlie's hair. He's just practically killed us both, but I've already forgiven him. You can't stay mad at Charlie for long.

From somewhere behind us, the Preston fans start singing loudly.

"We love you, North End!

We do.

We love you, North End.

We do.

We love you, North End.

We do.

Oh, North End, we love you!"

They're not being aggressive—just a bit noisy. Even so, most people on the carriage shrink into their seats or put on their music or pretend to be deaf. Charlie stares at them over the back of the next seat, grinning. I pull him down again before he gets us in trouble.

The fans start the chant again. And again. And again. Charlie turns to me. "Do you think they know any other songs?"

"Just ignore it," I say. I really like football, but Charlie doesn't get it. Dad took us to watch a game once, and Charlie spent the whole time under his seat playing cards against himself.

After the sixteenth verse of the same song, it's wearing a bit thin. One of the fans is stumbling down the carriage, red-faced and still singing. As he goes past us, Charlie calls out to him, "Excuse me."

My blood freezes. Charlie still hasn't grasped that we're supposed to be traveling under the radar.

The fan immediately stops singing and stares down at us. He's middle-aged with a big gut squeezed into a 1980s team shirt. Red face. Bald head. Glassy eyes. Bit rough-looking. He burps one of those deep, roaring belches that drunk people do to let everyone know they're there.

The train jerks, making him stumble forward, so he's leaning right over us and holding onto the seats for support. "What?" he growls. I can smell the booze on his breath. With his belly blocking my escape, I'm feeling extremely claustrophobic.

Charlie's smile doesn't fade, even though it's obvious that he's seriously misjudged this situation. "We were just wondering which team you love. We couldn't figure it out."

This is awful.

From down the carriage, the other fans have stopped singing.

The big guy grabs me—*me*, not Charlie, I'll just say

here—by the collar. "Think you're funny you . . ."

"Everything all right?" says a woman's voice from behind the guy's huge body.

He immediately straightens up and pats my shoulder a little bit harder than necessary. "Fine, officer," he says, his voice slightly slurred. "Just chatting about the game."

The police officer looks at me, her head tilted. I recognize her—she's the one from the train station. There's a long silence, and I realize she's waiting for me to agree or disagree with him.

"Like he says . . ." I whisper, the words barely coming out.

"Behave yourself or I'll put you off at the next stop," she warns him.

The man mumbles something at her and waddles toward the bathroom. When he's safely locked inside, I pull Charlie out of his seat. Still shaking, I lead him out of the carriage, past the closed bathroom door, and as far away from the North End fans as possible. I can feel the policewoman's eyes on my back as I go.

"He wasn't very friendly, was he?" whispers Charlie.

Ham and Jam

We walk for ages to find a seat. There's a whole empty table in the quiet car, but quiet places and Charlie don't really mix. Just as I'm about to sit down, he lifts his leg and lets out the biggest fart you've ever heard. I know you're not meant to be impressed by these things, but it *is* a seriously exceptional delivery and, with everyone else being silent, it rings out like a church bell.

"Whoa! Who cut the cheese?" booms Charlie, and a few people look at us and glare. I have to push him down the aisle, stifling my laughter and apologizing as I go.

We finally spot two empty seats in the next car right by the luggage rack and sit down. It's the last car before first class, and this time I get the window seat. Someone has left a newspaper and an empty paper coffee cup on the little foldout table.

Charlie plays bongos on the lid of the cup and twitches excitedly. "You know what? This is so awesome."

I put my jacket into the backpack and fasten it up again. "Just what we need." I smile.

It doesn't matter how nuts Charlie is or how many times he nearly gets us run over or beaten up. I just enjoy doing things for him. When he's happy, I'm happy.

The train races through a station. There's a brief blur of people on benches and graffiti-covered walls, then a smattering of houses before we're hurtling past green fields and bored cows again.

"I'm hungry," he says eventually. "Can I have one of those Christmas cookies now?"

"I told you," I reply. "They're for when we get there."

Charlie pretends to huff. "When's that?"

"Afternoon, maybe," I say. "What happened to the Jammie Dodgers I bought you?"

It's the kind of thing Mum would say, which immediately makes me think of her and Dad. My watch says seven thirty-five. They'll still be asleep. Dad didn't get in from work until late, so he won't wake up till elevenish at least. Then he'll be straight back down to the warehouse for the afternoon shift even though it's a Saturday. Maybe he'll stay on through the night if they ask him, which'll take him past ninety hours for the week again. And what time will Mum get up? Pick a time, any time, ladies and gentlemen. Twelve? Two? Tomorrow? Monday?

But then I have a terrible thought. Did I turn the alarm on my phone off? Shoot! If that goes off, it'll wake them up. Then they'll come into the bedroom. And then what? Suddenly, I'm gripped with worry. They'll see the train times of course. And the empty beds. And, downstairs, the space on the shelf where the special cookie tin should be. And my backpack missing off the hook. And the cereal boxes left open. And that jar I left empty and unscrewed. And . . .

Gotta relax. Gotta relax, I tell myself, the words following the rhythm of the train. We're on the move. We got through the tricky bit. It's not like they can come and get us, is it? I'm only jittery because I'm feeling guilty about leaving without telling them. It'll be worth it. We'll get to St. Bernards and be home before they know it. They might not even realize we left in the first place.

"I don't have the Jammie Dodgers," says Charlie. "I gave the rest of the pack to that homeless guy at the station just before you ran to the bathroom."

That's Charlie. He's a good kid. Even if his brain *is* inside out. I realize now why the homeless man gave me a thumbs-up.

"Can I go to the buffet car?" he pleads.

"No chance," I reply. There's barely anything in my wallet, and we've still got to figure out how to pay for somewhere to stay for the night. I reach into the backpack and pull out a squashed sandwich, even though there are still five hours until lunchtime. "Here. Have this. I made them last night."

"Ding-dong!" he says as he unwraps the cling film and looks under the top slice of bread. "My favorite. Ham and jam."

Yep. That's right. Ham and jam. On the same sandwich. He started eating them when he was two. Back then he just liked the way they rhymed, but it turns out they're delicious. Over the last year, I've even started eating them myself. When Charlie was little, Dad always used to tease him—*Do you want cheese and fleas next time? How about egg and leg? Chicken with sick in?*

"Can you time me, Marty?" says Charlie, dangling the sandwich in front of his mouth. Charlie loves to be timed doing anything. I start my watch, and he shoves the whole thing into his mouth. His cheeks are bulging out as his jaws work up and down. Finally he gives a painful-looking swallow, then opens his mouth and sticks out his tongue to show there's nothing left. Apart from some globs of liquefied sandwich that is. I stop the watch.

"Seven point two nine seconds," I say, impressed if a little disgusted.

"Oh yeah! New record!" exclaims Charlie, doing a little bum-wiggle dance in his seat.

I shake my head and dig into my sandwich. It tastes *so* good. Sometimes you don't realize how hungry you are until you start eating. When I've finished the first half, I wrap the other bit up and put it back in my bag.

I'm saving it for myself, but I'll probably have to give it to Charlie when he starts moaning again later.

"You still haven't told me why we're going to St. Bernards," he says, picking bits out of his teeth.

I yawn. It's been a long morning. "Something to do."

Charlie looks confused. "But we could do anything."

"Yeah but . . ."

"Do you think we'll see the dolphin?"

"Hope so." I shrug. It isn't time to tell him yet, so I close my eyes to show him the conversation is over. The gentle swaying of the car is so relaxing that within seconds I feel myself starting to drift and . . .

Dolphin

My eyes scanned the harbor to where Charlie was pointing. I couldn't see anything at first. But then I noticed it; on the surface of the sea, about 150 feet from where we were standing, darting in between the boats. A glimpse of fin. A hint of arched back. A light-gray shadow cutting through the water.

"Oh my God," I said. "Is that a shark?"

"Dolphin," said someone near me, but I didn't turn around to see who it was. My whole body was tingling and I felt like I'd been clamped to the ground.

The dolphin disappeared underwater, and we struggled to look for it between the boats. Then, after a few moments, its pointy nose poked up next to an orange buoy. Everyone by the railings cheered, and it set off again, slicing through the calm water. After a while, it stopped and bobbed up and down, showing off its white chest. Then, with a sudden explosion of spray, it burst up into the air.

Even today I can picture its leap perfectly, almost in slow motion—its body straining as it catapulted upward, showering down droplets of water that caught the sunlight like tiny flecks of gold. The way people gasped as it hung in the air. The slow, graceful turn of its body. The unexpected smash as it landed in the water, breaking the spell. The flick of its tail before it shot forward, out of the harbor and toward the open sea. That feeling of emptiness, grief even, when I slowly realized it wasn't coming back.

We stood there for ages, not speaking, before I eventually broke the silence. "Whoa," I said, puffing out my cheeks. "Just *whoa.*"

"Amazing," sighed Mum.

"Don't see them in Preston docks, eh, boys?" said Dad.

I didn't answer. And neither did Charlie. His mouth was hanging open.

Some Weirdo on the Train

My eyes open with a start. Was I asleep? Everything suddenly seems very different. Agitated and confused, I look around.

A girl is next to me, jabbering away on her cell phone. She's Indian, about sixteen, tight jeans, flowery perfume, and completely beautiful. I feel embarrassed like I always do when I'm this close to an older girl.

". . . no, it's not right. I'm not happy . . ."

Her accent's lovely—proper Midlands—*roight* . . . *oi'm* . . . *'appay.*

Hang on. *Midlands?* Where are we?

And where's Charlie?

The girl looks at me like I've just crawled out of a pond. "Do you mind?" she says. *Moind*—amazing. Then she shakes her head and mutters something under her breath.

Suddenly, I'm worried.

Where *is* Charlie? And hang on. Where is my backpack? Who's taken it? No. Not the backpack. Whatever happens. Not the backpack. It's got everything in it. I can feel panic squeezing around me like a boa constrictor and I frantically look under the seats but it's not there, so I pull on the girl's sleeve until she yanks it away from me.

"It was taking up the seat, so I put it on the rack," she snaps, pointing a sharp, pink thumbnail behind her, her hand over the mouthpiece. "I didn't wanna wake you up. You were . . . drooling."

How humiliating.

She looks me up and down with what? Horror? Pity? Then she goes back to her phone call. ". . . No, just some weirdo on the train. . . . Anyway tell me about this boy. . . ."

Some weirdo on the train. That's me. Five words that stab like little daggers under my ribs. And my brain is being yanked in different directions. The girl, Charlie, the backpack, and I spin around and scan over the back of the seat at the luggage rack and there's the backpack like she said. Thank God! But where on earth is Charlie? He hasn't left. He couldn't have left! But he's nowhere to be seen and the panicky feeling keeps growing and this girl's perfume is actually really strong and is it me or is the car just a little bit too hot and those lights are prickling away in my eyes again and . . .

"Tickets, please!"

A conductor's right there next to us and I'm all light-headed and wobbly and I don't know why but I stand up like a proper fool and I hold out the ticket and he stamps it and says we'll be in Birmingham in twenty minutes, which I guess is a good thing but only if I find Charlie and I feel a bit faint and now the conductor's looking at me and asking if I'm okay and I can hear my own breath inside my skull, which I guess is just a box of bone with your brain in it when you really think about it and the girl is staring at me too and she's standing up as well and saying ". . . This guy's really freakin' me out. . . ." and she's looking around for another seat and the next thing I know I've pushed past her and stumbled through the sliding doors in between the train cars and it's so clattery and rattly in there I've got to escape and get to the bathroom and I struggle through the next door and into the bathroom and slam the door and before I know it there's my chewed-up ham-and-jam sandwich staring up at me from the silver bowl.

My Brother

There was a young fellow named Martin
Who gobbled baked beans by the carton.
They went straight from his tum
Right down to his bum
And now he can't stop himself fartin'.

By Charlie Tompkins
Age 10

Stage 3b

Wolverhampton to a Shop at Birmingham
New Street Station

Distance—18 miles
Train and Walking

Poems and Puke

I've got serious jelly legs as I step through the automatic door back into our train car. My hair and face are soaking wet from splashing water on them, and I have to hold the wall for support. I feel totally relieved because Charlie's sitting there in my seat with the backpack next to him. He's writing in my notebook, his tongue sticking out of the side of his mouth as he scrawls huge, slow letters across the page. The conductor and the girl have both gone.

"What are you doing?" I say, a bit too harshly, as I grab the notebook from him. We're pulling out of Wolverhampton, which I know is close to Birmingham because we went past a sign for it on our way to Cornwall last year. Through the window, I can see the girl walking away along the platform. She doesn't look back, which in a funny way makes me feel better.

"Writing a poem," he replies. "Just like you. Hey! I

didn't know you write poetry, bro."

Saying nothing, I glance at his poem. It's a limerick about me and some beans. I might've found it funny if it wasn't for the panic, the throwing up, and the fact I'm trying to be angry with him for going missing.

"Don't ever disappear like that again," I say, slipping the notebook back into my bag. "I thought I'd lost you. Where did you go?"

"I was using my head," he says, tapping the side of his head. "I could see the conductor coming from right down the train, so I crawled onto the luggage rack and hid behind that massive suitcase. Didn't wanna wake you up. I know you get cranky when I do that."

"Huh," I say. Charlie's forever waking me up in the middle of the night to ask me some stupid question like *Why's mustard yellow?* Or *Why don't the pyramids have any windows?* I usually chuck a pillow at him.

There's a long pause as he studies my face. Finally he asks, "Are you feeling okay?"

I check that the cookie tin is still closed before fastening up my backpack again. "I'll live."

Puking up my sandwich on a train. Not normal.

Then again, these are not normal circumstances. I watch through the window as the train crawls past old warehouses and factories and strip malls and apartment buildings and endless housing complexes into the city. I need to sort myself out. In a few minutes, I'm going to have to figure out what we do next.

Tattoos

At Birmingham, the platform's packed. There's a low roof above us like we're underground, so I feel a bit claustrophobic. I hold on to Charlie's shoulder as we shove through the impatient crowd of people trying to get on our train. I'm not sure where we're going and I'm still confused and jittery, so I attempt to stand still for a moment. But then we're being jostled by people heading for the exit, so we have to push our way through to a bench by the side of the platform.

"What's the plan, boss?" says Charlie as we sit down.

I could really do with that piece of paper with the train times on it. Even though I know it's not in the backpack, I check one more time. If Mum and Dad find it, then they'll know exactly which trains we're on and then . . .

Probably best not to worry about that.

"Pretty sure we get a train to Plymouth next," I say,

looking at my watch. "And I think we've got a while to wait, but I can't remember."

I peer around, but I can't see a screen anywhere. While I'm doing that, Charlie reaches over and closes the notebook so he can see the cover. "Hang on! I didn't notice the dolphin picture before," he says. "It's one of mine! Where did you get it?"

I shrug, a bit embarrassed. "I cut it out of your pad and stuck it on, then I covered it with plastic. I thought it was pretty cool."

The notebook was just a plain, green school exercise book that Mr. Hendrix gave me for jotting down my poems. I wanted to jazz it up a bit. Charlie was always drawing pictures of dolphins when we were in St. Bernards last year, so they remind me of the vacation.

"That's amazing! I feel like a real artist." Charlie grins. Sometimes when he smiles he can't control himself, like the smile's taken over his whole face. Suddenly he clicks his fingers. "You know what? We should get matching dolphin tattoos in St. Bernards."

I laugh. There's no way anyone would give Charlie a tattoo. He looks about six years old. Then again, I'm fairly tall. *I* might pass for eighteen I suppose. On a good day. If the tattooist was shortsighted. "Actually that's not a bad idea. . . ." I say. A dolphin tattoo. *Perfect.* I wonder how much it would cost. Maybe I'd get a discount if the tattooist *was* shortsighted.

"Where will you get yours?" he asks. "I think I'll get mine on my face."

"Bit of an improvement. . . ."

"Actually, no. I'll shave my head, then get my whole body tattooed gray so I *look* like a dolphin."

"Your *whole* body?" I ask.

He seems to genuinely think about this. "Hmm. Good point. Why wreck something beautiful?"

I snort.

"Maybe I'll leave the rest of my body as it is and just have my willy done to look like a dolphin," he says.

"Ha! A dolphin?" I laugh. "More like a minnow! Or a shrimp."

At that moment, the football fans walk right past us along the platform, escorted by the police. I stop laughing immediately. *We're North End till we die* echoes passionately against the ceiling.

The fat one who grabbed me earlier is at the front, red-faced, neck veins bulging and hands clapping. He's looking straight ahead, so he doesn't see us. But that policewoman from Preston studies me carefully as she passes. There's a moment when I'm frozen on the bench as our eyes meet. Then she sweeps her gaze forward and she's gone.

"Let's go," I grunt after she's disappeared up the steps. Sitting still is not a good idea.

Dolphinwatch

By the harbor railings, Charlie had become totally hyped up. "A dolphin. Oh wow! Can you believe it?"

Dad waved his arm out toward the harbor. *"That's why you work hard for your vacation, right?"*

He was saying it half to us and half to anyone else who'd listen.

"Spot on, sir. Well said." An old man next to us grinned. He had bright-white hair, an open-neck shirt, and skin the color of walnuts. He pulled a cell phone out of his shorts pocket and began tapping away, muttering to himself in his rich, deep voice. "Seven twenty-five a.m.—bottlenose dolphin. In the harbor. Ten minutes, then left for open sea. Done."

When he looked up he smiled, noticing us watching him.

"What are you doing, old-timer?" asked Charlie.

Old-timer. Seriously?

"Sorry," said Mum. "So rude, Charlie."

The old man threw back his head and roared with laughter. "Not at all. Old-timer. Better than old git, I suppose. And, since you ask so pleasantly, I'm updating Dolphinwatch, my curious little fellow."

"Dolphinwatch?" said Charlie. "What's that?"

"Just a local website. It records whale and dolphin sightings along the coast here. A few of us post on it. Keep people informed, you know?"

"Let us look!"

Charlie pulled the old man's wrist down and began scrolling through the screen. The man didn't seem bothered, though. In fact, he shielded it from the glare of the sunlight with his free hand so Charlie could see it better.

"This 'un's been here pretty much twice a day for the last month or so," the old man said. "Really friendly, old girl she is. Big show-off. Last year we had four in the harbor at once."

"No way!" said Charlie.

"Way," said the old-timer, opening his eyes wide to show the white bits.

"So if we come back tomorrow we'll see her again?" asked Charlie.

The old-timer shrugged. "You might. If she's gonna come, she's usually here at high tide. Remember though—it ain't an aquarium, so you can never tell. Have a look on the tide charts to help you. All the best now."

With a casual wave, he strolled off in his flip-flops.

Charlie rested his chin on the railings and gazed out at the empty sea. "See you soon," he said. I wasn't sure exactly who he was speaking to.

Crime

The departure screen tells us there's almost an hour until our next train. Charlie needs a drink because his "mouth's as dry as a lizard's flip-flop," so we go up the escalators and along a wide passageway toward the main part of the station.

"Problem," I say.

There's a turnstile in front of us. You've got to feed your ticket into a machine before it'll let you out, but we've only got one ticket. I consider trying to make it through while holding on to Charlie, but there are guards everywhere keeping an eye out.

"You wait here and don't move," I say to Charlie. I don't want to leave him on his own, but I don't have a choice.

"Cool. I'll look after the backpack." He grins. "Wouldn't mind cracking open those cookies."

I clutch the backpack to my chest. Since we've been off the train, I've had it on my front so no one could take it. "Definitely not!" I snap.

Charlie takes a step backward. "Wow! What's bitten you on the bum?"

"I told you. We're saving them till we get to St. Bernards."

"All right, all right," he says, his voice high-pitched. "I heard you the thousandth time. Keep your knickers on."

I take a deep breath. "Look. I'm sorry. I'm still a bit . . ." I begin but I don't want to finish. "I'll get you something nice."

I squeeze his shoulder and lead him over to the wall. He sits down on the floor; then I head through the turnstile.

You can tell Birmingham's a big city as soon as you step out into the main part of the station; it's massive and jazzy and completely awesome. Light pours through the high glass arches of the ceiling. There are screens, shops, restaurants, and Charlillions of people scurrying everywhere and bustling past me. It's a bit scary if I'm honest but I've got a job to do, so I take a deep breath and step forward. Gripping the backpack even more tightly, I stride toward a store where the snacks and drinks are in a fridge right by the open doorway.

Some of the drinks aren't too expensive, but when I check my wallet, I've only got eight pounds and eighty-three pence left. I've no idea how that's going to last overnight, especially since now I'm going to see if I can afford a tattoo in St. Bernards as well. How much do hotels and tattoos even cost?

An idea crosses my mind. A stupid one, I know. There's a security guard at the door, looking brainlessly out across the station. I gulp. This is *so* wrong. I can't. I don't do stuff like this. But, then again . . .

In the end, the decision is a surprisingly quick one. *Just do it and do it now*, I tell myself. *Do it for Charlie.* I casually walk along the fridge aisle, pretending to inspect the sandwiches and salads while slowly unzipping my backpack.

A quick peek around the fridge toward the entrance. Security guard yawning. Behind me a lifeless shop assistant is rearranging a basket of bananas.

Now!

As nonchalantly as possible, I stroll back along the aisle, my face saying, *Nope, there's nothing here for me.* When I get back to the drinks at the end, I look over to the security guard one more time. He's checking his watch and stretching his neck left and right before lazily waving at someone across the forecourt. It has to be now. I bite my lip. *I shouldn't. I shouldn't. I shouldn't.*

But I do it anyway.

I reach forward, grab a massive bottle of orange juice, then slip it into my bag and zip it up in one motion. Shouldering the bag, I march out as quickly as possible, around the corner of the shop. I take one last look behind me, then—

Whack!

I stumble backward. The backpack hits the ground.

Oh nuts.

I've walked straight into a bright-yellow jacket.

And *even worse*, it's that stinking policewoman again.

I gulp. "Sorry, sorry, sorry."

"Oh hello," she says, picking up the backpack, which sloshes guiltily at her. "You again?"

I try to say hello back, but my voice sticks in my throat. She's not too much taller than me, and she's got a warm smile that I didn't notice before. Behind her, the football fans are being escorted toward the station exit.

"Rail replacement buses," she says, nodding her head backward and weighing the backpack up and down in her hand. "Engineering works. Pain in the neck. Where are you off to, then?"

I want to lie, but I can't think of anything. "St. Bernards, Cornwall," I whisper, staring anxiously at my backpack as it dangles from her hand. *Don't open it, please.*

Her eyes widen. "Wow. Long way. Why are you going there?"

Questions. Questions.

For what feels like ages, I stand there spluttering, trying to think of something to say. Why *am* I going to St. Bernards? What am I doing? What's the point of any of this?

I'm worried I'm starting to look like a suspicious character, so eventually, I blurt out the first thing that comes into my head. "I want to get a tattoo."

Oh shut up, you complete idiot.

She looks at me for a moment, like she's trying to figure me out.

I have to fill the silence. "Best place to get them, St. Bernards. It's a fishing village, see, and everyone knows that fishermen have tattoos and loads of artists live there too, so it's bound to look good and . . ."

This is awful. She narrows her eyes at me. Suspicious character? More like a total freak.

Then she sniff-laughs through her nose and shakes her head. "Okay, then. Well, gotta go. All the best with the tat. Don't do anything you might regret. Oh. And I hope you're old enough."

My head nods up and down like a bobblehead.

After handing me the backpack, she pauses for a

moment, as though she's about to ask me one more thing. My throat tightens. Then she seems to think better of it and turns around before striding toward the exit.

Does this mean I've gotten away with it?

I'm not going to hang around to find out. My belly is going nuts, like a washing machine full of milkshake. Quickly, I hurry back to the turnstile.

Happiness

Standing on a beach
Sand beneath your feet.
Swashing orange juice
Through your teeth.
Dancing alone
In a crowded room.
Free music playing—
Boom *chinga* boom.
Happiness is easy to find.
But you can lose it in a moment.

By Martin Tompkins
Age 13

Stage 4a

Birmingham New Street Station
to Just Past Bristol Temple Meads

Distance—About 90 miles
Train

Reggae

I slip back through the turnstile and find Charlie sitting cross-legged on the floor where I left him. His lazy eye is closed, his palms are pressed together like he's praying, and he's making an *ommmmmm* sound.

"Is your belly button laser getting flat again?" I ask.

Charlie opens his eye. "Nope. Just trying to figure out the meaning of life and . . . hang on . . ." He shuts his eye again. "*Yep.* Got it."

"So what is it, then?" I snort as Charlie leaps to his feet and dusts off his hands.

"What's what?"

"The meaning of life."

"Ah. Well, actually, it turns out it's . . ." he says, leaning in toward me, ". . . cheese."

I run my hand through my hair. Is he serious? "The meaning of life is *cheese*?"

"Yep. I was surprised too." He shrugs. "Makes sense,

though, I suppose. Anyway, did you get us a drink?"

I shake my head and hand him the juice. He glugs it, rinses it through his teeth, then gargles before swallowing. I take a nervous sip and shove the bottle into the backpack before anyone sees.

The relief of not being caught has been replaced with a suffocating mega-guilty feeling. Honestly, I have never stolen anything before, so this is a really big deal for me. Then I remember the *special-left-over-from-Christmas* tin that I stole from the house. And when you add that to not buying Charlie a ticket for the train, that makes three crimes committed in one day. And maybe kidnapping as well. So that's four. Actually, is it illegal to run away from home? Or to pretend to be an adult when you're not?

Yikes.

I'm a serial offender.

Right away I make a decision. As soon as we get home, I'm going to send a card to the shop to say sorry for taking the juice. I'll get ahold of some money and seal it inside. Maybe I'll put in a couple of pounds extra and tell them to donate the change to charity. This makes me feel better.

We check the screen, find out where the Plymouth train is leaving from, and walk along the passageway toward our platform without speaking. A street performer is playing slow reggae on a battered acoustic guitar. He's shaking his dreads and singing about lazy days at the beach with the sand beneath his feet. He's pretty good, his thumb and long fingers gracefully slapping the string—*boom-ching, boom-ching*—eyes closed and his voice all mellow and distant.

As we get closer, Charlie nods his head and snaps his fingers. Then he just starts dancing in the middle of the station. And not *normal* dancing either. Dancing like he's having a fit or something. Flinging his arms and legs around, waggling his head with his tongue hanging out, attempting to do head spins and the worm.

It's pretty funny in a Charlie kind of way because he's totally out of time with the slow rhythm and he's so uncoordinated—kind of like a drunk baby donkey being electrocuted. Plus, no one seems to have noticed him, which makes it even funnier. People are just stepping around him the way people seem to do in big cities, staring dead ahead or down at their phones, and the musician's eyes are still closed, so he can't see him either. But now Charlie is completely wigging out, leaping up and down and head-banging.

I'm about to start laughing when I hear a "Hey you!" from behind me.

My heart freezes.

Two policemen are jogging down from the other end of the station, thirty feet away and getting closer. Tight short-sleeved shirts. Big muscles. Angry faces.

Oh no.

They know about the orange juice.

I'm a wanted man.

I grab Charlie, but the police are closing in on us and I shut my eyes and squeeze him and that shaky feeling is growing inside me again and I make a whining noise and wait for the handcuffs but . . .

"You know you need permission to play music here," growls one of the policemen.

"Come on. Beat it," says the other. "This is twice today."

I open my eyes, and they've got their broad backs to me, crowding the musician toward the wall. I feel relieved for a minute, but then I see the man's face and I feel sorry for him. His frown seems to show anger, confusion, fear, and disappointment all at once.

"Leave it out, man," begs the musician in a strong accent. "Haven't you got any criminals to catch?"

Trying to stay dignified, he stuffs his guitar into its case, then pockets the coins from his woolly hat.

"Don't get rude with me, son," snaps the first policeman. "I could take you in for breach of peace."

The musician sucks his teeth as he balances the hat on top of his dreads. "Police," he says, with every ounce of hate in his body. "All I'm doing's making people happy."

"Well, you can make us happy by going home," says the second policeman, easing him along by his shoulder.

As they pass, I catch the man's eye and give him a thumbs-up to say I liked the music. He returns it with a sad smile. "See that?" I hear him say to the policemen. "People like my music. The world needs more joy and you're stealing it. You're nothing but happiness thieves, man."

Toilets and Tickets

The Plymouth train is completely crammed. There are people standing in the aisle with suitcases and bikes everywhere. I only manage to find a window seat at a table of four. Right away, I find out that beggars can't be choosers.

At my table are the following people:

An old woman diagonally across from me who cleans her false teeth with a little brush and a cup of water before sticking them back into her gums. Then she picks up the cup of water and swirls it around. It's all cloudy with bits of food floating in it. Finally, and I promise this isn't a lie, she downs it in one large gulp. Gross.

An enormously fat, sweaty man right next to me. His bare arms are touching my bare arms, and I can't escape. He's watching a funny movie on his iPad with his earphones in. I only know it's a comedy because he keeps laughing really loudly, his whole body shaking up and down. Sometimes after a big laugh, he turns to me, eyes tearing up, and shakes his head as if to say, "Wasn't that great?" *How should I know, man? I can't hear it.*

The angriest-looking girl I've ever seen. Huge backpack on her knees, blue hair, multi-colored wool coat even in this warm weather, pierced eyebrow and lip, and a *come on, I dare you to look at me* glare burning on her face. She's sitting right across from me in the other window seat, and I'm really doing my best not to catch her eye.

Charlie, by the way, is in the bathroom. When the train left Birmingham, the announcer said they'd just gotten a new conductor on board so they'd be checking every ticket. Charlie was actually delighted when I told him to hide in the bathroom and not to move until I came for him. Told you, he loves a good toilet.

I keep thinking about the musician. He's given me an idea for a poem, so I start jotting it down in the notebook. But it's hard to concentrate because of the wheezy fat laughter, and the clicking false teeth, and

Angry Girl, who's trying to read what I'm writing. I glance up at her and she gives me a proper death stare, so I cover the notebook and finish as quickly as I can.

Mr. Hendrix told me to find a cool, calm, peaceful spot to write poetry. This train is definitely not what he had in mind, so I don't think the poem's got much going for it. I mean, it starts out okay, but I end up rhyming *room* with *boom chinga boom*, which is completely lame (and in any case I'm not sure the station *is* considered a room). Also, I rush the last line a bit, so it ends up having a sad ending.

I know Mr. Hendrix would be like, "Hey, don't sweat it. A true poem is always better than a good poem." But was this poem true? Why did I need the weird last line? I suppose it's because of how the police just stopped the music like that. I wish Charlie was here. He'd have come up with something funnier.

Actually, scratch that. I'm way better off with Charlie in the bathroom. By now he would've said something inappropriate about the fat man, or tried to tickle Angry Girl, or asked the old woman if he could borrow her false teeth or something.

Thinking about Charlie wearing the old bird's false teeth makes me smile to myself.

"*What?*" snaps Angry Girl.

"Nothing," I mutter, and I lean back into my chair. This is going to be a long journey.

Classic Economy Budget

After the dolphin had disappeared, we headed off to find a café. All of us were in a great mood, and of course Charlie was the most excited of all of us.

"Did you see her?" he was saying, his eyes wide and the words shooting out like sparks. "The way she just flipped up like that, I've never seen anything like it, I mean, she was just *alive*, you know?"

"Of course it was alive," laughed Dad. "I doubt a dead one'd swim quite so fast."

Mum gave Dad a soft slap on the shoulder. "*I* know what you mean, Charlie. But just don't get too excited. You know what the doctors say."

Charlie's meant to avoid getting overstimulated, just in case his heart beats too fast. Even though he's had millions of tests and scans and checkups, the doctors still aren't sure exactly how strong his heart is. *It's impossible to tell. He could live until he's a hundred, or, well . . .*

Probably shouldn't think about it really. I mean, Charlie never does.

Charlie waved his hand at Mum like he was batting away her words. "But it was the most mega-magic thing I've ever seen." He grinned, practically bouncing up and down. "It was like a . . . a . . . a beanie full of hope and happiness."

"A what?!" cried Dad as we stopped outside a place called the Sandy Bottom Beach Diner. "Well, *I'm* wearing a baseball cap full of hunger. Let's all get in here, calm down, and get some bacon and a drink. . . ."

Inside, we each had a full English breakfast— bacon, sausage, eggs, mushrooms, tomatoes, beans, and toast—apart from Charlie, who ordered three fried eggs on top of a bowl of porridge, just to see if they'd make it for him. They did, and we were all treated to the sight of it sloshing around in his mouth as he relived every millisecond of the dolphin's appearance again and again.

When Charlie had finished his breakfast, which according to him "tasted of the future," he made us all eat up; then he dragged us down to the harbor to see if the dolphin had come back. Unfortunately, the tide was heading out by then. The fishing boats that'd been floating around an hour or so ago were lying tilted in the shallow water, and the harbor walls were slick with seaweed. Of course the dolphin was long gone.

Charlie stared out at the sea for a while, quietly scanning the horizon. There was no sign of a fin or even a splash. Disappointed, he made Dad take a photo of a blackboard with all the tide times for the week on it so we'd know when to come back. As we walked away toward the car, he kept glancing over his shoulder as though he expected the dolphin to come slithering up onto the sand any second. It didn't.

For the twenty-minute drive out of town, Charlie was pretty quiet for a change. He sucked his thumb as we whizzed out through the suburbs, then along narrow country lanes. In fact, he didn't perk up until we pulled into the RV park. There was a massive sign as we drove in: "Surfside—One Life—Anything's Possible."

"I like that," Charlie remarked as Dad parked outside reception.

As soon as Mum went to the office to collect the keys, Dad turned around in his seat to face us. "Okay, boys," he said, "I'll warn you. The RV might not be the nicest one in the park. . . ."

From the brochure we had at home, I already knew that Surfside was a pretty massive place that backed onto a beach about seven miles along the coast from the main town of St. Bernards. As well as a pool, and a game room, it had around six hundred RVs and cottages of all different shapes and sizes. There were some sweet brand-spanking-new accommodations, but we'd booked a "Classic Economy Budget" RV, which is a fancy way of saying *Old, Cheap, and Crap.*

Dad stroked his stubble and cleared his throat. "We needed to save a bit of money so we could do more stuff while we're here," he said apologetically. "Better to sleep in a cave and live like a king than sleep in a palace and live like a beggar, right?"

I got the feeling he'd been working on this line for a while. "We don't mind," I said, shrugging my shoulders. I mean, a vacation's a vacation, isn't it? I didn't care where we were staying; I had this quiet, buzzing, excited feeling in my belly, and I couldn't wait to get unpacked and get the vacation started properly.

But Charlie stared at the big Surfside sign for a few moments. "I'm going to help Mum," he said. Then he hopped out of the car and ran over to reception.

They were gone for ages. Dad sat resting his head on the steering wheel, and I stayed in the back, eating some warm, squashed Starburst left over from the night before. After about ten minutes, they came back to the car. Charlie had a big grin on his face, and Mum was looking a bit confused.

Closing the door, she handed a map of the park to Dad. "They've drawn a circle around where we're staying," she said. "We're in the red zone, right by the sand dunes."

Dad stared at it for a moment. "Hang on. That's not right. We should be in the brown zone. It says here that the red zone is for Deluxe Premium Sea-View Cottages."

I raised one eyebrow. "Deluxe Premium" is a fancy way of saying *Ultra-Fancy Super-Expensive*. I glanced over at Charlie, who was deliberately looking out of the window.

Mum shook her head. "I know. We got upgraded."

"Upgraded?!" cried Dad. "Well, you can just go back in there and *down*grade us. I'm not paying another five hundred pounds for a fancy kitchen and a nice view."

Mum put her hand on his arm. "No. You don't understand, love. It's free."

"You what?"

Still looking out of the window, Charlie casually said: "I just asked if they had any spare. Turns out they did."

"They aren't fully booked this week," explained Mum. "And they've had some cancellations, so there are quite a few empty. They said they wouldn't normally do it, of course, but Charlie charmed them. . . ."

"Don't ask, don't get," said Charlie.

Dad spun around to face him. "What? And they just gave one to you like that? For nothing?"

Charlie looked at him with his head tilted to one side. "Well, I had to sing to 'em first."

"He's not kidding either," said Mum. "They were like, 'How can we refuse after hearing that?'"

I felt a giggle tickling my throat. "What did you sing?"

"'If I Was a Rich Girl,'" Charlie said, totally deadpan.

"Were you any good?"

Mum shook her head. "Absolutely. Awful. I think they only upgraded us to shut him up."

There was a moment of silence before we all broke out laughing.

Charlie didn't laugh, though. He just smiled. "Anything's possible," he said to himself. "Anything's possible."

Fat Men and Toilets

Along with most of the other people on the train, the fat man finally gets off at Bristol. *Relief.* His heavy-metal T-shirt, from a band called Monkey Apocalypse, clings to his body along with a kind of musty, damp odor. Charlie would've said the smell was the mold growing under his man boobs.

The old woman gets off too. She's spent pretty much a whole hour eating a single salmon sandwich with tiny sparrow bites. It was gross. Her false teeth clacking up and down and her mouth full of mashed-up fishy paste. Why did she bother cleaning her teeth if she was just going to eat a sandwich right afterward?

Anyway, when she stands up, the fat man grunts, "Hurry up, Mum," and I realize that they're traveling together. This is really weird. They haven't said two words to each other the whole way. In fact, they haven't even looked at each other since we left Birmingham.

I suddenly think of my mum. *We* don't really talk much these days either. I hope I don't end up like the fat man when Mum's old—lost in a trance and totally ignoring her.

Oooh. He'll miss her when she's gone. That's what Mum would say if she was here. I just know it.

I feel my stomach sag. Somehow, the idea of the old woman dying and the fat man missing her makes me feel sad. I make a mental note to talk to Mum more when I get back tomorrow. You can't take people for granted.

Mum.

Is she out of bed yet? Has she realized we're gone? Is she upset? Has she noticed the missing cookie tin?

The last one makes me smile sadly to myself, and I tap my backpack to make sure the tin's still there. It is.

Hmm. Maybe I should just send her a text to let her know we're okay. I reach for my phone, but then I remember it's still in my open drawer at home, which in turn makes me regret making it so obvious that we'd run away. I wish I could go back in time and clean up after myself: alarm off, drawer shut, cereal box away, train times in my backpack, cookie tin back on the shelf (keeping the cookies of course), lid back on that jar.

It's too late to do anything about all that now, though. I can't go back and change anything. I have to look forward. As for Mum, I'll get in touch once we've done everything we need to do in St. Bernards.

Thinking of families, I remember that Charlie's been in the bathroom since Birmingham. As the train pulls out of the station, I pick up the backpack and wander down to him. The aisle is empty now, and it feels weird walking in the opposite direction of the way we're going. Am I going backward or forward or just standing still? I knock on the door, and there's a swooshing noise as it slides open. Charlie's sitting on the toilet seat, looking surprisingly happy.

"Has the conductor been around yet?" he says, jabbing the close-and-lock button.

I let him have a big glug of the stolen orange juice, then drink some myself. "No. The train's been too busy. I'm sure he'll be along soon. I'll come and get you soon as he's gone."

"No rush." He grins, waving his arms around to show

the space. "I've got the best seat in the house. Look at this leg room."

"But it stinks," I say, then tuck the juice bottle back into my bag.

Charlie shrugs. "I'm used to it. I've been sitting next to you all morning, remember. Anyway. I'm starving. Can I have a cookie now?"

"I told you," I say, rolling my eyes, "when we get there. Now get out. I need to use the facilities."

As I—ahem, you know—*go*, Charlie's jabbering on in my ear the whole time. It's a wonder I don't get stage fright.

"Hey, do you remember the bathroom in the cottage at Surfside? It was like a palace."

I smile at the memory. "And it was the only room we could get a phone signal," I say over my shoulder.

"Yes!" chuckles Charlie. "I'd forgotten that. I spent hours in there, checking Dolphinwatch on Dad's phone."

"Mum said if you stayed in there any longer someone'd use you as a toilet brush!"

Charlie laughs so much he has to take a puff of his

inhaler. Mum's got a great sense of humor when she's in the mood, you know? I guess that's just Charlie's influence. He brings out the best in everyone.

Then Charlie's face turns serious. "So . . . since going to St. Bernards was your idea, have you been checking it, then?"

"Checking what?" I say, zipping my trousers up, then turning around.

"Dolphinwatch."

I wash my hands and dry them under the pathetic air dryer. "Of course I have. Every day since last year. You know that."

Checking Dolphinwatch was something I got in the habit of after our vacation had finished. It's a bit strange that it's me who does this. I mean, it was Charlie who was into looking at it when we were actually *in* St. Bernards. But he gets bored easily, and I just felt like I should keep checking it once we'd gotten home.

When I turn to face him, his eye is wide open. "*And . . . ?*"

I try to look innocent. "And what?"

"Is she back?" he asks, half pleading now.

"Is who back?" I say, playfully flicking water at his face. I'm determined to drag this out as long as I possibly can.

"The dolphin, you muppet!" snaps Charlie. "Has she started coming back to the harbor or not?"

"Maybe," I say. I ruffle his hair and wink at him as I slip back out into the train car.

Sand Dune

A Shape Poem

My
brain's
a sand dune,
thoughts like tiny
jumbled grains of sand
piled up into a hairy mountain.
And sometimes the weight of it becomes
too great so that one of the grains slips and tumbles,
dislodging others and dragging them downward in a chaotic,
swirling mini-avalanche that temporarily changes the shape of everything,
until later, when a gentle gust of wind eases across the dune, filling the holes
and smoothing out the drifts until the dune is reshaped and peaceful once again.

By Martin Tompkins
Age 13

Stage 4b

Somewhere Just Past Bristol
to an Alleyway by the Side
of a Cheap Hotel in Exeter
via Exeter St. Davids Station

Distance—About 80 miles
plus around 984 feet
Train and Sprinting

Kick in the Shins

I'm feeling pretty pleased with myself as I saunter back down the train. I bet Charlie's going nuts in the bathroom right now.

Ever since we left the house this morning, I've been waiting for the right moment to let him know about the dolphin. According to Dolphinwatch, it disappeared during the autumn and winter, but then it came and went through the spring and summer. But it's been back every day for the last few weeks, so the time's right for us to go. High tide's at seven this evening. We'll get in at five-ish, so we should have plenty of time. Of course the ocean's not an aquarium, but still, I just *know* the dolphin's going to be there.

The happy feeling doesn't last long. As I slip back into my seat, I realize that Angry Girl is reading my poetry book. She's folded the page right back, and she's just reading it like she owns it. I must've forgotten to put it in my bag. *What an idiot.* Without thinking, I snatch it away from her.

She raises her eyebrows in surprise, then fixes me with this strange look that I can't quite understand. Her dark lips are pursed, and she's gazing hard at me. Is she mad at me for taking back my own book? Or is she poking fun at my poems?

Either way, I decide to ignore her and look out of the window. I don't feel bad about grabbing the book off her. The poems are mine. No one else is allowed to read them apart from Mr. Hendrix. What made her think she had the right? Immediately the train shoots into a tunnel. The noise and the sudden darkness make me jerk my head away from the glass. Angry Girl smiles, which doesn't suit her face. Why are some people such idiots?

There's a light kick on my shin. I move my leg to the side, but she does it again.

"You all right?" she asks.

I shrug.

"Interesting poems."

I don't answer. Like I care what she thinks?

"Where you going?" It's more a challenge than a question.

Still I say nothing. The pressure from being under-ground rises in my ears.

Another kick when we burst into sunshine again. "Come on. Tell me. Where you going all alone?"

I can't place her accent. It seems a bit posh. Maybe Devon? And her face and voice are so unreadable that I can't tell if she's making fun of me. For the first time, I actually look at her. She's probably about seventeen, but she's small and thin so she could easily be three years older or three years younger. She'd be pretty if it wasn't for the crazy coat and the stupid blue hair and the aggressive eye makeup.

Okay, so there are quite a few barriers to her being in any way likeable. Not that looking good is all that counts. I mean, a personality is just as important as being beautiful. Unfortunately, it seems like she might be missing one of those as well.

This time she boots me really hard. "Don't be rude, answer the question."

Rude? I think kicking someone is a bit ruder than ignoring them.

"St. Bernards," I say, doing my best not to wince. Hopefully she'll leave me alone now.

"Cornwall? Oooh, very nice," she trills. "Might go there myself."

"Oh. Right." *Like I honestly care.*

"Wanna see something?"

Not really, I think. I'm just about to ask her to go and bother someone else when she loosens her backpack, pulls out a large plastic bottle, and dumps it onto the table with a thud. "Pretty cool, eh?"

The plastic isn't see-through, so I can't tell what's inside. Grinning smugly, Angry Girl spins the bottle around and points to the label. A few of the words jump out at me.

PARAFFIN. CAUTION. HIGHLY FLAMMABLE.

She snaps her fingers, and, as if by magic, a lighter appears in her hand. "Imagine," she says, licking her lips and slowly turning the flint with her thumb. "One spark from this and KABOOM! No more train."

My head is light and I feel like I'm looking down on

the train car from a long way up. I don't like it. Not one little bit.

Angry Girl slides it proudly back into her bag. She looks delighted to have scared the pants off me. "So you'd better be nice."

There's something really unsettling about the way she says this. It's almost friendly and almost threatening, and the way she stares at me for a little bit too long afterward. . . .

What is she? A pyromaniac? A terrorist? *Got to get away.*

Grabbing my backpack and making sure I've got my poetry book this time, I wobble nervously to my feet and stumble down the aisle. I want to change train cars, but then I realize I'm heading the wrong way. This is the front of the train. There's nowhere else to go. Just a locked door and a sign telling me not to distract the driver.

Oh God.

I turn around. She's still in her seat. At least she hasn't chased me yet. But I'm not going past her again. No way. I look around. *Think. Think.* I could pull the emergency lever, but it says there's a fine of 250 pounds for improper use. Would this be improper use? I don't know. But I *do* know I haven't got 250 pounds.

Maybe I'll tell the conductor when he comes along and only use the brake if she follows me. *Good idea. Take it easy. She hasn't moved yet.* I plop into the sideways-facing seats that are near the exit doors. When I sit down, I take several deep breaths and try to keep it together. I'm about ten rows away from her, I think, and if I stand up, I can just about see her. Unfortunately, Charlie is still in the bathroom down at the other end of the train car. I figure out a plan. At the next stop, I'll get off, sprint along the platform, and get back on again farther down the train. Then I'll hide in the bathroom with him until we reach Plymouth.

This plan relaxes me a bit. Eventually I feel brave enough to see what Angry Girl's up to, so I peer over at her. The way that she's looking out of the window, all moody again, makes me think she might not be about to follow me. I'm all right for now. As long as I stay calm that is.

It's okay, I tell myself. *Write a poem. That'll help. No. Even better,* read *your old poems. You won't get carried away then. You can keep one eye on her.*

The notebook automatically falls open on the third or fourth page, which must be where she'd folded it back. It's one of my first poems from last year, right from when I started poetry club. It's a pretty weird one about a sand dune. Only it's not about a sand dune. It's about my brain. I remember that I didn't want to show it to Mr. Hendrix at the time. As soon as I'd finished it, I'd slammed the notebook shut. He just said, "No problem. I understand. Sometimes the poems you write reveal something that catches you by surprise." When I finally allowed him to read it a few weeks ago, he patted me on the back, then flicked ahead to my more recent stuff and said, "Look how far you've come."

Personally, I didn't think the sand dune poem was all that bad. But still, that doesn't mean I wanted Angry Girl to read it.

Hairy Mountains

When we drove around to it, the cottage didn't disappoint. It was a beautiful log cabin nestled among some pine trees. Inside was even better. An airy, open-plan kitchen and living area, and three bedrooms (even though Charlie said he preferred to share with me). There were leather sofas, a great big television, a sound system with a dock for your iPod or phone, and even an Xbox.

But that wasn't the best thing.

The whole back wall of the living room was made up of these patio doors that kind of folded back on each other. Through them was a wooden balcony with a table and chairs and our very own barbecue.

"Oh wow!" exclaimed Charlie, leaning over the balcony railings. "Hairy mountains."

"They're sand dunes," I said, rolling my eyes.

Topped with spiky, green grass, the dunes stretched

in a ragged line across the back of the row of cottages. The balcony was perfectly placed so you could see the ocean framed between two of them.

"It's gorgeous," whispered Mum, joining us on the balcony.

"You should sing more often, son," said Dad.

But Charlie didn't reply. He was already climbing over the railings. "Race you to the top!" he called to me, leaping off the side of the balcony and landing on the sand three feet below.

"Careful!" Mum called, but he was off. "Go after him, Martin. Make sure he's okay!"

Doing as I was told, I followed him. Charlie was halfway up the dune by the time I got to the bottom, but I soon overtook him, my feet sinking deep into the fine sand. I collapsed at the top, my thighs and lungs burning, but I hardly noticed. I was looking out on the most amazing sight—a huge arc of golden sand curling off for miles in both directions. Hundreds of people were sunbathing, playing on the beach, and surfing or bodyboarding through the huge, white breakers. Over to the left, the harbor and white cottages of St. Bernards poked out from behind a rocky outcrop, tiny and hazy in the distance.

"Check that out," I gasped, but when I turned around, Charlie still hadn't joined me. He was lying on his back halfway up the dune, wheezing and spluttering.

"You okay?" I said, sliding down on my backside to meet him.

"*In-ha-ler,*" he wheezed, clutching his throat and jabbing his thumb toward the cottage. His eyes were round with panic and his face was bright red.

"Oh nuts!" I exclaimed, and I half ran, half tumbled down the dune to get help.

Poems and Announcements

It takes a long time before I convince myself that Angry Girl isn't going to blow the train up. For a while, she looks out of the window, occasionally flicking her eyes toward me. Then she takes out a book, shoves her backpack up on the shelf above, and starts reading. Amazingly, she even manages to read angrily, flipping the pages over like she's trying to hurt them. I'm relieved her paraffin is out of reach, and I feel myself starting to relax.

Soon, the conductor comes along from the back of the train and asks for her ticket. I hear Angry Girl say something that sounds like, *"Non capisco inglese."* It could be Spanish or Italian, but it might be total gobbledygook. She's frowning at the conductor like she's no idea what he's talking about. The conductor repeats himself slowly and tries to draw a ticket in the air.

"*Non capisco,*" she says again, shaking her head apologetically and sounding out every syllable. "*Mi dispiace. Sono una straniera.*"

"I said. Ticket. Now. Or no travel. Understand?" the conductor says.

He's beginning to lose patience with her, but she seems not to notice and just nods happily back at him. "*Grazie mille, signore.*"

With this, he gives up. As he walks along the carriage toward me, he tells her over his shoulder that she'll be getting off at the next station. Angry Girl blows him a kiss.

She's clearly a total lunatic! And an armed one at that. I should definitely tell the conductor about how she threatened to blow up the train. And how she's only pretending to be foreign. As I'm handing him my ticket, I say "Excuse me," but at that moment, his phone rings.

"Sorry, gotta take this," he says, giving me back the ticket without looking at it before bustling his way back along the train and chatting into his phone. "Remember. Off next stop," he says to Angry Girl as he passes, putting his hand over the receiver.

"*Ti amo anche,*" Angry Girl calls after him.

I take a deep breath, put my notebook back in the backpack, and slip it onto the floor for safekeeping. *Everything's okay. She'll be off soon; then I won't need to worry.*

An announcement over the speaker suddenly breaks my thoughts. "Ladies and gentlemen, we will shortly be arriving at Exeter St. Davids," says the crackly voice, which I recognize as the conductor's. "If there's a Martin Tompkins from Preston on board, please could you make yourself known to the police at this station?"

I freeze.

The police!

Why do they want me?

Is it about the orange juice?

Or has Mum called them?

Whatever. This is not good.

As the train slows, Angry Girl strolls along the train car in my direction, backpack over one shoulder. I catch her eye, which feels like a mistake. She must notice the panic on my face because I can tell that she's realized it was *my* name that was announced.

When she passes, she leans in toward me and whispers, "Quick tip: Try not to look so obvious. Don't let them know who you are."

I'm still trying to figure out if she's actually being kind as the train begins to creep into the station. The platform we're stopping at is on the other side of the train from my seat. Two police officers, a man and a woman, are standing there, watching the train come in and talking to a guard. There's a dull, heavy feeling deep in my gut as we inch past them. I ignore Angry Girl's advice and scramble across the aisle so I can get a better look. Finally we squeak to a stop.

For ages, the train doors don't open. Have they stayed locked for a reason? From somewhere down the train, I can hear someone jabbing at the button, then swearing when it doesn't work. Pressing my face against the window, I can just about get the angle to see back along the platform. Our conductor has stepped off the train and has joined the police officers and the guard. They're about a hundred feet away, level with the middle of the train.

The policewoman shows the conductor a piece of paper. He squints at it, rubs his chin, then wags his finger toward our train car. The police officers follow him along the platform. I want to run, but there are a couple of people standing in the aisle.

Stay calm. Don't let them know who you are.

I sit, frozen, trying and failing to look casual. My eyes follow the conductor and the police as they walk along the platform and past my window. Now they're at the doors right next to me. The conductor takes out a kind of T-shaped key, plugs it into the side of the train, then turns it. There's a clunk-hiss as all the doors on the train open at once. I can see that the piece of paper in the policewoman's hand is a photo. *A photo of me?*

It's too late. They know exactly who I am.

I don't have time to think. The people trying to get off are shuffling awkwardly to one side of the car so the conductor and the police can squeeze past.

All except Angry Girl that is.

"Ciao, bello," she says, placing her hands on the conductor's chest.

"Not again. . . ." he moans.

"Excuse us, please," calls the policeman from behind him.

But Angry Girl refuses to budge. As the conductor tries to shift her out of the way, she turns to me. "Go!" she urges, yanking me out of my seat with her free hand. "Run!"

In a split second, I've made my decision and I'm wriggling out of the seat and back along the train, away from the police and past a couple of people in the aisle and there's an old guy in front of me putting on his coat but I manage to shimmy around him while the police are calling behind me but they struggle to get past Angry Girl and I'm in the clear along the aisle and out through the next set of doors, barging off the train past the people trying to get on, and I have a quick pause on the platform to find the exit sign, then I'm up over the footbridge two stairs at a time with my feet slapping the ground and down the other side and someone's yelling for me to STOP NOW and another guard gives a puzzled glance at me as I run past, but before she can react, I'm out of the station sprinting past a line of taxis, looking over my shoulder but there's nobody following. I turn left then right and then right again and the next thing I know I'm leaning against a wall down the side of a hotel, retching and spitting and trying to catch my breath.

It's only then that I realize I don't have my backpack. And I don't have Charlie.

Lost

A Chant

Lost in a strange town
I sat and cried
Cause I realized I'd lost you
And lost something inside

Repeat again and again

By Martin Tompkins
Age 13

Stage 4c

The Alley by the Side of a Cheap Hotel in Exeter
to the Worst Car in the World

Distance—30 feet
Walking

Pains and Memory Loss

I don't know how long I've been squatting here, leaning against the wall and rocking backward and forward.

The only thing I *do* know is that when I realized I didn't have Charlie and the backpack I blacked out big-time, maybe the second-worst one ever, and it felt like my brain was spurting out all over the place like lava from a volcano. I must've been screaming or something because I remember that someone (an old woman?) came down the alley to see what was up but I waved her away, howling like an animal. In my head, I can just about picture her terrified expression, but when I think about it, her skin peels off, her eyes turn dark red like a zombie's, and she begins clawing at my face. I know this didn't happen. I think it's just my brain going wacko again because it can't deal with the sudden shock.

A few minutes go by.

I'm feeling exhausted from the panic attack. It's been ages since I've had one. I should've known it was on the way, what with the mini-meltdown at Preston and the puke on the train and the *stress* of everything, but it's still hit me hard and fast like a ninja.

At least they always pass. Even the bad ones. And now I'm starting to return to the real world again, aware of the sharp, cool bricks against my back, and the aching thirst in my throat, and the raw throbbing of my knuckles. I wish I had that bottle of orange juice. The thought of it makes me lick my lips.

I notice a thumping pain in my head, and when I open my eyes, I have to squint against the dim sunlight of the alleyway. There's an overflowing trash can across from me, and I'm surrounded by a really strong smell of toilets. When I look at my knuckles, I see they're shredded and bleeding, and I can't really bend my fingers. Maybe I punched the wall like I did that other time this happened. Who knows?

For a few minutes, as I slowly come around, I flick in and out of consciousness. Behind the hum of some traffic noise, I can hear trains pulling in and out of the station, and suddenly I'm flying above the train as it rattles along through the countryside, then I'm zipping into the train car through an open window. And there's the backpack, under the seat where I left it. And I float down the aisle, past the handful of bored passengers and into the bathroom where I can see Charlie. He's happy and unaware that anything's wrong and I want to hug him, but when I reach for him, he disappears like he's made of mist and I'm back here in the smelly alleyway before I know it.

I feel sick about Charlie. *What kind of a brother . . . ?* I know I was panicking, but come on—there's no way I should've left him behind. How can you lose a person? I'm not even meant to be here in the first place. And now there's no way I can get to him, or the backpack. *The backpack too.* How stupid can I get?

This is a real disaster. I was only trying to do the right thing, but it's all collapsed. *What have I done?* My shoulders shake, my fingers dig into my eyes, and I begin to sob.

Surprises and Phone Calls

I cry and cry, and a rhyme starts to form in my mind. It's about being lost, but I can't get past the first few lines. They're on an endless loop. It's a silent chant: *Charlie's lost. The backpack is lost. I'm lost.* In more ways than one.

Gradually I become aware of someone else here. Don't know how. I didn't notice any footsteps. It's just that feeling of being watched. I brace myself. Is it the police? I guess I'll have to hand myself in. I don't have the stomach to run again. And they might have to find Charlie and the backpack for me. But then I'll have to go home and I'll have to answer to Mum and Dad. The whole trip will have been a waste of time.

I move my hand away from my eyes and feel my body jolt. Of all the people in the world, it's Angry Girl who's squatting in front of me, holding a bottle of water in front of my face.

"Have you taken something?" she says. Her voice is much softer than before.

I gulp. "A bottle of orange juice. From a store in Birmingham," I croak. "But I'm gonna pay for it, I promise."

After a few seconds, I realize she means *drugs*. Just being asked this question makes me feel weird and I don't like it. Not-So-Angry-Anymore Girl cracks up, but not in a nasty way. I'm surprised how concerned she looks, even when she's laughing at me.

I take a glug from the bottle; then she pours some of it onto my knuckles and dabs them gently with a tissue.

"Why were the pigs after you?" she asks finally.

I've only been back in the real world for a minute, so I have to shake a weird picture out of my head of giant pigs chasing me down the train. "Ran away from home," I say finally, wincing from my stinging fingers. I can bend them so at least they're not broken. "Me and my brother."

She stands up and looks around, adjusting her massive backpack. I'm surprised how this news doesn't surprise her, if that makes sense. "Parent trouble?"

"Sort of," I say.

"Huh," she says. "Tell me about it. A little young for running away, though, aren't you?"

"We're only going for a night."

"Fair enough. Make them sit up and notice, anyway. As long as you stay safe. Where's he, then?"

"He's hiding in the bathroom on the train," I say. Suddenly I'm gripped by an urge to *do* something. "I've got to get back on the train to meet him. And I need to get my bag."

I stand up way too quickly and get a massive head rush that makes me stagger back against the wall. Angry Girl grabs me by the shoulders and looks at me through her heavy eyelashes. "You're not going anywhere. I was watching you freaking out just now, from the street. I dunno what all that was about, but the train's long gone and *you* need to take it easy for a while. And anyway, you go back to the station and who do you think'll be waiting for you?"

"You don't understand," I say, brushing her hands away. "The bag's really important. I can't lose it. I *can't.*

And Charlie needs me. And it's all my fault and—"

I try to push past her, but she stands in my way. "Is your brother stupid?"

Her question stops me. "No."

"Then he'll stay on the train until Plymouth and wait there till you show up, won't he?"

"Well. Maybe," I say. I suppose it makes sense. He knows that's where we're heading. It's always been a rule in our family: if you get lost on the way somewhere, wait at the destination. You need rules like that when you've got a liability like Charlie running around. But then again . . . "What if he heard the announcement on the train and he got off here? He could be wandering around the station looking for me right now. He'll be lost and alone and he needs me."

Angry Girl weighs this up. "All right. I can go look for him in a minute. But first we need to do something about your bag if it means so much to you." She pulls out her phone. "What kind is it?"

I describe it to her while she's doing a search on her phone; then she taps the screen and holds the phone to her ear. "Ooh, hello there, dear," she says after it's rung a few times. The sudden change in her accent is amazing. She sounds just like an old Scottish lady. "Is that the Plymouth Station manager? You won't believe it, I've made a silly, wee mistake and left my backpack on the train at Bristol. . . ."

After Angry Girl's arranged for my backpack to be taken off of the train by a member of the staff at Plymouth, and for it to be collected from the station by her granddaughter (giving a perfect description of herself by the way), she hangs up.

"Taken care of," she says, pleased with herself. When I look confused, she explains, "If I'd said it was yours, they might not have given it to me. The police are looking for a lanky kid who got off at Exeter, not a *wee old Scottish lassie who hopped off at Bristol*, remember."

Even when she's putting on the accent again, she still sounds seriously businesslike. The way my brain's still buzzing, it feels nice to have someone who can take charge, even if I don't really know who she is, or whether I can trust her or not.

"But how are we gonna get to Plymouth?" I ask, which is just one of the millions of things that are making my brain ache right now.

Angry Girl smiles. "You let me worry about that. Now, I need to know what your brother looks like."

Anything's Not Possible

By the time I'd legged it back to the cottage, Dad was already vaulting over the balcony rail, holding Charlie's inhaler, while Mum climbed down behind him. We sprinted back up the dune together and stuffed the inhaler into Charlie's hand. He took a few puffs of it before slowly catching his breath.

Dad rubbed his back. "You've got to be more careful. You know you can't go running off like that without your inhaler."

Mum was nervously rubbing the little, gold crucifix she wears around her neck between her finger and thumb. "Oh God, I thought—"

Face like thunder, Charlie ducked away from her hand and stumbled angrily down the sand dune on his own. Halfway down, he turned around. "It's a stupid, crappy lie!" he shouted.

"What are y—?" began Mum.

"The sign!" snapped Charlie. "Anything's *not* possible! Just when you think . . ."

His voice trailed off, and he stormed away again. After struggling to pull himself up the balcony railings a few times, he stomped away and disappeared around the side of the cottage. A few seconds later, we heard the front door slam.

I wanted to go after him, but Dad said to let him calm down and the three of us sat on the soft sand together for a while, not saying anything.

Eventually, we followed him back. Inside the cottage, the bathroom door was locked and Dad's phone had gone from where he'd left it on the kitchen table. It was weird how quickly things had changed: the excitement of seeing the dolphin, the buzz of the cottage, the panic of Charlie's asthma attack, and now this.

For the next hour, the bathroom door stayed closed. The rest of us unpacked and wandered about barely talking to each other. Charlie's mood was like a blanket over a parrot's cage, subduing and silencing the rest of us. After a while, Dad went off to the store to get milk, but I didn't fancy going with him. I was desperate to be out on the beach. Bored, I switched on the Xbox, but I couldn't get into it, so I chucked the controller down on the sofa and marched over to the bathroom. I'd had enough.

The Worst Car I've Ever Seen

When Angry Girl comes back twenty minutes later, I don't realize it's her at first. This is because she's in the passenger seat of a car that pulls up at the end of the alleyway.

"No sign of anyone who could be your brother," she calls, rolling down the window. "So hurry up. We need to get a move on!"

I tentatively walk over. This is honestly the worst car I've ever seen. It's an ancient VW Polo. The passenger door and roof are red, but the rest of the car is a kind of dirty cream, except for the huge rusty holes at the bottom of the bodywork. And the massive permanent-marker picture of a skull and crossbones on the roof that looks like it was done by a hyperactive four-year-old.

The driver is a youngish guy with no shirt on. He's skinny, with loads of tattoos all over him. His head is shaved, and he's wearing those dinner-plate ear-rings that stretch out his earlobes. I'll be honest—I'm terrified of him. But then he leans forward in front of Angry Girl and gives me a toothy grin. "Hear you need a lift," he says in a friendly Devon accent. "Hop in."

My hand reaches out for the rear-door handle. Then I stop. What am I doing? I don't know this weird man with the dangly earlobes. I don't even know Angry Girl. This whole thing's making me nervous.

"Don't wanna rush you, old boy," says Dangly Lobes, "but we're in a no-parking zone and I ain't rich enough to pay parking tickets."

"We want to get your brother, don't we?" says Angry Girl, and I don't know why but I trust her. I know it's wrong and stupid and against every sensible bit of advice you could ever be given, but what other choice do I have? Charlie and the backpack are gone. I can't go back to the station, and I'm completely broke. I can't get the backpack unless Angry Girl collects it for me from Plymouth, and I can't get to Plymouth without climbing into the car. It's not like I've got any other options. But still, I don't move.

Angry Girl hops out and stands really close to me. Her voice is low and secretive. "Look. Your poem. The one about the sand dune. It was . . ." She blows a strand of hair out of her face. "It was like . . . reading about *myself*. Like you'd been inside my head or something. . . ." She pauses to swallow. "When you were having trouble with the police, I just had to help you, and then, when I saw you in the alleyway, well . . ."

Still unsure, I look at her for a few moments. It's not too long ago that I thought she was going to blow me up.

She seems to know what I'm thinking. "I'm sorry about when we were on the train. Sometimes I find it . . ." She frowns, like it's a real struggle to push the words out. ". . . hard to be nice."

The look she gives me then is so surprisingly kind and unguarded that I find myself biting my lip and climbing into the car.

Not

That funny looking kid's not weird or stupid,
He's just different.
And this pen isn't a pen,
It's a key that opens up hidden doors.
And that dolphin isn't a dolphin,
It's a magic creature that changes people.
I guess what I'm trying to say,
Is what you think and what things actually are
Can be two very different things.

By Martin Tompkins
Age 13

SUCKS!

Stage 4d

The Alley by the Side of a Cheap Hotel in Exeter
to Plymouth Station

Distance—45 Miles
Car

Cakes and Old People

During the first fifteen minutes of the car journey from Exeter to Plymouth, I learn the following things:

Angry Girl is actually named Henrietta, but I should call her Hen because "Henrietta's the kind of name you give to a canal boat."

Her dad, who she hasn't seen since she was seven, is Italian, which is why she was speaking Italian to the conductor on the train. She tells me that, at one point, she'd actually told the conductor that she loved him! She never buys a train ticket, and this is her favorite way of not getting busted for it.

Dangly Lobes is actually named Wesley, although most people call him Doctor Lizard for reasons that aren't really clear.

Doctor Lizard, or Lizard for short, is Hen's best friend, and he'll do anything she asks, although they are definitely not boyfriend and girlfriend. They grew up near each other in Exeter and like hanging out and going to music festivals together. Whenever she's in town, she sleeps in the spare room at his parents' house.

Lizard's car is called "the Tank." I thought the outside was bad, but the inside is even worse. There's no carpet and that rusty hole in the floor is so big that I can see the road under my feet. The seat is scarred with deep gouges, like it's been attacked by a panther. Black smoke pours out of the exhaust the whole time, and the engine rattles, shakes, and whines as though it's in pain.

Lizard works as a caregiver in an old people's home. This doesn't seem to fit with his crazy image, but after a few minutes of knowing him, he seems to be a very nice person.

According to Hen, the old people at the home love him. In fact, when he got sacked for teaching a seventy-eight-year-old woman with two false hips to skateboard, the rest of the residents refused to eat until he got his job back. When he came back to work, Lizard celebrated by baking scones for all of them. Henrietta says that Lizard is *amazing* at baking. This is another thing I wasn't expecting to learn about him.

As soon as Hen mentions baking, Lizard tells me to fish out a tin from behind his seat. I reach down and open it. It's filled with delicately decorated cupcakes with swirly blue icing and silver balls sprinkled on top.

"Made a batch for one of the old boys. It was his ninety-second birthday," he says, smiling to me in the rearview mirror. "These are the leftovers. Help yourself."

They look awesome, but it's really funny; he'd be the last person in the whole world you'd expect to have made them. This just goes to show that you shouldn't judge people by what they look like. It reminds me of a poem I wrote once about how we look at things. I didn't like it at the time, so I crossed it all out and scrawled "Sucks!" across the page. But it makes sense now I guess. Mr. Hendrix wouldn't let me tear the page out of my notebook. He said that poetry's about emotion, and the scribbling shows I was frustrated and angry at the time, so it's actually kind of cool to leave it as it is. I like Mr. Hendrix.

"I keep telling him to go on that television show *The Bake Off*," says Hen, but Lizard grins and shakes his head.

I take a cupcake and quickly hand the tin to Hen. I don't want to hold on to it for too long because it makes me think of the *special-leftover-from-Christmas* tin in my backpack, which in turn makes me think of Charlie.

I bite my lip, but strangely enough, I don't freak out again. I think this is for three reasons. Firstly, no matter how bad the car might be, I know that we're moving toward Charlie. Hen was right. My brother might be crazy, but he's definitely not stupid. I know he'll be waiting for me when I get there. I just know it.

Secondly, I'm a lot less stressed after what happened in the alleyway. Like I wrote in the sand dune poem, everything seems calmer when the avalanche is over. In fact, I feel a bit floaty.

And thirdly, well, the cupcake is ridiculously delicious, and there aren't many situations that can't be improved with a cupcake, right?

"Why do you need to head to Plymouth then, fella?" says Lizard, steering the car with his wrists and unwrapping his cupcake at the same time. We're way out of Exeter now and we're on this open land, bleak and empty. There's a part of me that thinks this would be a perfect place for two weirdos to take a stranger they've just kidnapped so they can murder him, but I shove this thought down before it takes over.

"Told you on the phone, he's lost his brother. And he needs his bag," says Hen. She snatches the cupcake out of Lizard's hands, unwraps it for him, then shoves it into his open mouth so that he can steer properly.

Lizard chews the cupcake and swallows but doesn't say anything.

I fold up the cake wrapper and shove it in my pocket. Of course this is a waste of time. The car is littered with old take-out wrappers and drink cans, but I don't feel right dropping garbage in his car when he's doing me such a massive favor.

"Thanks for taking me," I say. "I appreciate you going out of your way."

"'S all right," replies Lizard, picking his teeth. "Hen rings me up out the blue and says, *Take me to Plymouth, boy.* I'm only working mornings this week so I say,

171

All right, why not go on a bit of a mission, eh? I'll pop in and see my nan while I'm there. No bother to me if you hop in too. More the merrier, I say."

I feel myself frowning. This doesn't make any sense. If Hen had wanted to go to Plymouth in the first place, why didn't she stay on the train? That's where it was heading after all. She'd have gotten there way quicker if she hadn't gotten off. Okay, I know the conductor had told her off for not having a ticket, but she didn't exactly look scared of him. And in any case, on the train she'd said she *might* go to St. Bernards.

"I didn't know you were going to Plymouth too," I say to Hen.

"Just decided when we got off the train," she replies. "Was gonna stick around in Exeter for a few days but—"

Lizard interrupts her. "Did your mum know you were passing through town?"

"Drop it, Wesley," she says, running her hand through her hair. I notice the way she uses his real name. The atmosphere in the car suddenly feels tense.

"Well. Just saying. I saw her in the store last week

and she said she ain't seen you in four months and don't know if you're alive or—"

"I said drop it," she snaps.

"Ooh," jokes Lizard. "Someone's tired."

Hen shakes her head and half laughs. "You're an idiot."

"You just *suddenly decided* to go to Plymouth?" I say, blurting out the question before I can stop myself. The post–panic attack wooziness seems to stop me from holding things in.

"Oh, didn't she tell you?" says Lizard cheerfully. "Bit of a wild one, our Hen."

"Stop it," says Hen, but her voice is playful, not angry, now.

"All set to go to art school last year. Then what does she do? Quits school just before her exams."

"I left," mutters Hen. "Don't like being tied down."

Lizard taps the steering wheel. "You can say that again. Goes wherever the wind takes her. Then shows up back here whenever she feels like it."

Hen sniffs. "Nothing wrong with seeing a bit of the

world. And anyway, if I stay in one place too long, the police get to know my face. And that isn't what I want, trust me."

I gulp. Why doesn't she want the police to know her? *Is* she a terrorist? Or a murderer? What the heck am I doing in this car with her? The feeling that this was a bad idea comes flooding back. The speedometer is jiggling around at about fifty miles an hour. For a moment, I try and figure out what will happen to my body if I open the door and dive out.

Lizard glances up at the mirror and seems to notice my worried expression. "Ha. Don't worry. She ain't a criminal. She's a *juggler*."

"A juggler?" I say.

Hen is too busy squirming in her seat with embarrassment to answer me, so Lizard speaks for her. His voice is extremely enthusiastic. "Oh yeah. Best 'un I've ever seen. Just shows up in a town. Juggles away. Draws in a crowd. Few coins in the hat. Then does one before the coppers catch her. Dunno why they don't like her, though. Doesn't do any harm far as I can see."

"They don't like anyone different," mutters Hen.

"Tell you what, though," continues Lizard, slapping the steering wheel for emphasis, "you should see her with them fire sticks. She really scares me, man. I swear she'll go up in flames one day."

"It's paraffin," she says matter-of-factly. "Doesn't burn too hot. Looks worse than it is. Sorry for scaring you with it on the train by the way. Just trying to break the ice."

A juggler. Of course. What a relief! I laugh to myself. I feel a bit foolish for thinking she was going to blow up the train.

I try and relax and look out of the window at the open land. I'm really starting to feel like maybe everything might be okay. . . .

Dolphin and Chips

"Hey!" I said, banging on the bathroom door. No answer. Mum told me to let him be, but I wasn't having it. "Stop ruining our vacation and get out here. You promised Dad—being miserable wasn't an option, remember?"

"Leave me alone," replied Charlie.

I took a deep breath.

"Aw, come on," I begged. "We're supposed to be having fun. Look. We'll do whatever you want."

I didn't know if this was true or not, but I had to try something.

"Anything?" he replied finally.

I looked over at Mum, who was putting dishes away in the kitchen cabinets. She nodded. "Yes," I said.

The bathroom door opened slowly. Charlie was standing there with Dad's cell phone in his hand and a sly grin across his face. I smiled. He was back. "What do you want to do, then?"

"Fish and chips for dinner," he said cheerfully, as though nothing had just happened. "Back in St. Bernards. The seafront. Seven o'clock tonight."

"Is that it?"

He nodded.

"And you promise to stop spoiling everyone's fun?"

He saluted solemnly. "Brownie's honor."

For the rest of the afternoon, we went to the site's outdoor pool, which was pretty sweet. It had slides and inflatable rafts, and me and Dad played volleyball with a family from Wales. Charlie didn't join in. Mum thought he should rest after his asthma attack. At first, he was a bit fed up about it, but Mum bought him a pad from the store and he sat at a plastic table and drew pictures of dolphins, which seemed to keep him entertained. When I got out, I told him they were amazing, even though they had that scruffy, babyish look that all Charlie's pictures have. Charlie grinned, extremely pleased with himself. It's rare for him to sit still for that long.

At exactly twenty past six (Charlie was determined

we left on time), we piled back into the car and drove into St. Bernards. Dad got annoyed because he didn't want to drive again, but Mum told him we'd promised Charlie and that was that. He soon cheered up, though, because Charlie was back to his excitable self, firing out jokes like torpedoes the whole way there: "Did you hear the one about the man with five willies? *No.* His underpants fit him like a glove."

And so on and so on.

When we got to St. Bernards, Dad and I went to the restaurant while Mum and Charlie found a bench. It was crowded in the restaurant and all along the walkway. The evening was warm and clear, and it seemed like everyone in town had the same idea. Finally we got to the front of the line, grabbed four trays of chips and a couple of fish to share (a complete rip-off, according to Dad), and wandered along the front to find Mum and Charlie.

The tide was in again. Out to sea, the sun was beginning to set, and a rippling, golden path stretched across the water from the harbor wall to the horizon. The air was sharp with seawater and vinegar.

When we found Mum and Charlie, they weren't on a bench. Charlie was standing on the bottom rung of the railings, with Mum next to him. They were part of a group of people staring out to sea.

"She's back!" Charlie cried, bouncing up and down. "I knew she would be back and she is! Look!"

As if he'd called it over, the dolphin cut through the water right in front of us, skirting the harbor wall right by our feet. Up close it was so beautiful: a gray shadow ringed by a glistening halo of water.

"Yes!" cheered Charlie, leaning out between the bars. "Yes! Yes! Yes!"

Mum had to pull him back by the sweater. "Calm down, Charlie. I don't want you having another attack."

So we stood by the railings, eating our chips and watching the dolphin as it glided around and around the bay, sometimes dipping down for a few minutes, then popping up somewhere else, sometimes hissing out a cloud of spray as it eased past. It was amazing how much happiness it gave people. Everyone was clapping and hollering as it passed them.

Once, it stopped just thirty feet in front of us, its

head nodding up and down, a wide smile and sharp little teeth visible over the gentle waves, a crackling, squeaking noise coming from its throat.

"Oh wow! Oh *wow*! She's looking right at me!" cried Charlie. And then, without warning, he grabbed Dad's portion of battered cod and threw it into the sea. It landed with a splash and sank under the water. The dolphin ducked its head and followed it down.

"Ha-ha! Go on, girl!" cried Charlie.

Dad was furious. "What'd you do that for?"

"Easy," said Mum.

"That's four pounds worth of fish," protested Dad. "I hadn't even had a bite."

"The dolphin looked hungry," said Charlie to Dad. "Here, have you got any ketchup to go with it? She might be a fussy eater."

Mum and I giggled.

"I'll turn you into ketchup if you're not careful," said Dad, but he said it in a kind of not-so-mad-anymore way that made Charlie smile. "Right. Finish your chips and let's get back. I'd like a beer from the fridge."

"Awww," begged Charlie. "Just ten more minutes."

"No," said Dad firmly.

But Charlie refused to move. In fact, we ended up staying for nearly an hour. Even though we loved watching the dolphin, Mum, Dad, and I got a bit bored after a while. Plus, it was getting darker and cooler, and by quarter past eight, we were all shivering and we could barely even see the dolphin anymore.

In the end, Dad had to pry Charlie's fingers off the railings and drag him away. Even then, Charlie made him promise that we'd come back at least once a day for the rest of our vacation to see the dolphin again.

And we did.

Drop-Off and Search

There's a line of buses outside Plymouth station (more rail replacement issues, I guess), so Lizard drops us off as close as he can and says he'll do a spin around the block and see if he can find somewhere to park.

I thank him and climb out. Hen looks around and takes off her multi-colored coat. "Put it on," she says to me. "The police can email your photo to every station in the country. Doesn't take much to confuse them, though. Trust me."

Even though it's really warm for September, I do as she says and follow her over to the station entrance. She walks quickly, making me keep a gap between us. As I follow, I wonder what made her quit school and start juggling for a living, running around the country, dodging the police, and never seeing her mum. And I wonder why she pretends to be so angry when she's actually really nice and kind.

We reach the entrance, which is a pretty dreary place, a low 1970s building next to a big apartment building. It's even more depressing when I see that Charlie isn't waiting for me outside. But then I think it through. Why *would* he be here? He'll be expecting me to come from the train, so he'll be on the platform. I know it.

The inside of the station is surprisingly nice, with white tiles on the floor and these cool sail-shaped things underneath the glass roof. It's quiet, and there's still no sign of Charlie. Luckily I can't see any police either.

"Go and wait over there. There's a chance that this is a setup and they know it's your bag. If you see any cops, run, all right?" says Hen, pushing me toward a rack of tourist leaflets. I flick through one about an aquarium, but really I'm peering over the top of it for Charlie.

A couple of minutes later, Hen comes back. She hands me my backpack. I check inside—the cookie tin is still there, which is awesome beyond words. The bottom of the bag's a bit damp and sticky, so I guess the juice has leaked, but that doesn't matter. "Thank you so much!" I say.

"No worries," she replies. Her phone beeps and she reads the screen. "Lizard. He's parked somewhere he shouldn't be, so he's not gonna stick around. I'll run and get my stuff from his car. You find your brother. I'll meet you on the platform, and we'll sort out a plan."

I tell her to thank Lizard for me as she darts out of the station. But as soon as she's gone, I start to feel uneasy. What did she mean by *a plan*, exactly? I thought she'd help me get the bag and Charlie and then we'd go our separate ways.

Hmmm. I'll figure this out once I've found my brother. There's a bored-looking guard standing by the turnstile. "Excuse me. What platform did the last train from Birmingham come in on?" I say, as confidently as I can.

She frowns. For a moment, I think she must know who I am, but then she says, "Platform six, love."

I feed my ticket into the machine and sprint up the stairs, along the bridge, and follow the sign down to platforms five and six. I run down the steps as quick as I can, then search for Charlie. There are a few people scattered around the platforms, reading papers, drinking coffee, and messing around with their phones, but I can't see him anywhere.

Just as I'm starting to feel worried, I notice a bench at the far end of the platform. There's a small boy sitting there. Confused face. Scruffy hair. Baggy sweater. Thick glasses. Peppa Pig eye patch.

"Charlie!" I shout.

He looks up and gazes around. I call again and wave my arms like crazy, and eventually he peers toward me. A grin slowly spreads across his face.

My Brother Charlie

A Recognition

Tiny fighter
Crib biter
Inn keeper
Dreadful sleeper
Walrus flopper
Card dropper
Cottage upgrader
Cookie-tin raider
Sandwich rhymer
Dune climber
Patch wearer
Bedroom sharer
Asthmatic wheezer
Little geezer
Dolphin watcher
Now I've gotcha!

By Martin Tompkins
Age 13

Stage 5

Plymouth to Somewhere Else

Distance—Not sure how many miles
Train

Hugs and Rolos

I sprint along the platform and dive onto Charlie, giving him the biggest rib-crushing hug ever.

"Gerroff!" he says, but he's laughing his head off and I don't want to let him go ever.

There are tears running down my cheeks, and I'm digging my nails into his shoulders, hugging him tighter and tighter. I'm crying like a baby, but I honestly don't think I've ever been so happy in my life. "I'm sorry," I say. "I'm so, so sorry."

"That's nice," he croaks. "But I think my lung's just collapsed."

Snuffling and giggling at the same time, I let him go, slap him on both shoulders, and have a look at him. "I'm so glad you're okay."

"Where did you disappear to?" he asks. "I looked everywhere for you. I've been sitting here like a lonely penguin."

"Didn't you hear the announcement on the train about the police?" I asked. "It's been . . ."

I can't finish the sentence, though, because I'm crying again and I've got to cover my eyes and clench my teeth together for a few moments.

"No, I didn't," he says. Then there's a pause and his eyes sparkle with excitement. "The police? *Cool!* Are we wanted men?"

I swallow and take a deep breath, then wipe my face with my sleeve. "Sort of. But it's fine. I think. I had to run away but I was in a rush so I forgot you and the bag and I'm so sorry, honestly . . ."

I'm about to cry again, but Charlie waves his hand. "Forget it. What was all that you were saying in the train toilet about the dolphin? Is it really back?"

"Yes!" I say. "It's back, and we're going to see it, I promise."

"I knew it!" exclaims Charlie, clenching his fists and shaking them excitedly. "We should celebrate. Look at this; I found a couple of Rolos on the train when I came out of the bathroom. Bit squashed and warm, like someone had been sitting on them, but still . . . amazing what people throw away. Would you like one?"

He holds them up to me. They're flat as pancakes, and they're not even wrapped. *Gross!* I shake my head. Charlie shrugs, then chucks them both into his mouth.

"Cool coat, by the way," he says, the Rolos slopping around in his cakehole. "Did you rob a thrift store? Is that why the fuzz are after you? And, *hey*, what happened to your hands?"

"I borrowed the coat from a friend. And I had an argument with a wall," I say, but the mention of the police makes me uneasy. "We should get moving. The next station we need's called St. Something-or-other."

"St. Something-or-other," he says, pushing his specs up his nose. A trickle of Rolo juice dribbles out of the corner of his mouth. "Is that near Who-Knows-Where-Ville?"

"There'll be a schedule somewhere. I'll know the place when I see it written down," I say, thinking yet again about the piece of paper in my room with the train times on it. "It's about two hours away I think.

We can change trains there, and it's about another ten minutes after that. Not long now, I promise."

"And then we'll get to St. Bernards?" he says.

"Yep."

"And then we'll see the dolphin?"

I look up at the station clock, five to three, and bite my lip. "Hope so."

"And then I can have one of the *special-leftover-from-Christmas* cookies."

"We'll see."

At that moment, there's a shout from across the tracks. "Martin!"

I look over. At first, I tense up in case it's a policewoman, but then I can see Hen. She's standing opposite us on the next platform.

Charlie's face hardens, and he narrows his eyes suspiciously. "Who's *that*?"

"Hen," I reply, waving over to her.

"I'll come over!" she calls, pointing toward the stairs. But our view of her is blocked off by a long, sleek train that rolls slowly up to our platform.

"I don't like her," says Charlie.

"Huh?" I reply, totally surprised. "But you don't know her. She helped me get the bag back. And she got me a ride. I wouldn't have found you if it wasn't for her."

The train squeaks to a stop, and a door clunks open right in front of us.

"Don't care. Come on," says Charlie, dragging me toward the train by the hand. "We're getting out of here."

"What are you talking about?" I say, confused. This isn't like Charlie at all. "She's our friend."

Charlie stares angrily at me. "No she's not. Let's go. Now. She'll just get in the way."

He releases my hand and storms onto the train. "This is nuts," I call after him. "You don't even know where it's going."

But Charlie is already sitting down in a seat, and the train doors are beeping like they're about to close. I look along the platform. I can see Hen's feet as she jogs down the stairs. Now her shins. Now her legs.

The doors hiss at the exact moment that Hen reaches the platform.

I feel like a horrible person, but I can't afford to lose Charlie again. Turning away from Hen and hoping she doesn't see me, I dive through the doors just before they close.

Hooked

"You can tell it's a good vacation," said Dad, "'cause everyone has a big smile on their face."

He was right. The vacation was *amazing*. After that first day, we didn't stop beaming the whole week. On Sunday and Tuesday, we went to the beach. I tried bodyboarding and Charlie buried Dad in the sand while Mum sat and read her new book. Monday we went to Lands' End; then we played miniature golf back until it got dark. Wednesday was a theme park (where me and Dad went on a roller coaster and Charlie managed to lose a shoe on the tea-cups ride), followed by a completely amazing monster-truck extravaganza in a park outside St. Bernards.

Somehow, along with all of that, we still managed to get down to the harbor every day to watch the dolphin. Dolphinwatch and the tide timetable ruled everything: a stop off in St. Bernards on the way to or from somewhere, a quick ride out in the car at lunchtime for Mum and Charlie, while Dad and I played in the sea or played football back at the cottage.

Charlie was happiest when he was down at the harbor. He'd stand, mesmerized, watching the dolphin skim around the harbor for as long as we'd let him. Sometimes he'd be pressed against the railings, sometimes drawing or taking photos with Mum's camera, sometimes chatting to the old-timer from Saturday. But always there'd be a massive grin plastered across his face.

On top of that, Charlie spent hours learning about dolphins, finding out facts on the internet on Dad's phone, drawing pictures of them in his little pad. He even made us go to the local library so he could read books about them.

Yep, the dolphin had changed him all right. Mum said she'd never seen him concentrate for so long. As the week went on, even his drawing and coloring improved—instead of his usual messy, multi-colored scribble, he'd take his time, carefully sketching then following the lines with his felt tips.

Everything was perfect.

Until Thursday.

It was a wet day, and we'd been to visit an old mine, which was a lot more fun than it sounds, creeping around deep underground in the dark. Once, Dad hid in this little alcove and jumped out at us, but Mum told him off and said he'd scare Charlie if he wasn't careful. While we were in the museum afterward, Charlie suddenly announced it was time to go. High tide was at four o'clock, and we'd promised.

At the harbor in St. Bernards, sheets of drizzle were shrouding half the bay. To be honest, the rest of us were a bit bored with the dolphin now, so we huddled under a shelter by the side of the lighthouse with a flask of tea while Charlie paced up and down the railings in front of us, peering through the rain.

After fifteen minutes of us watching Charlie watching the sea, there was still no sign of the dolphin. Dad called out to him: "Come on, son! It's pouring. You've seen one big fish, you've seen 'em all."

Without turning around, Charlie replied that, actually, dolphins are mammals. He was starting to look agitated now, and he shoved fifty pence into a telescope. Ten seconds later, he stepped off the little platform again, muttering about how useless it was.

"Well, what did that old fella say the other day? It's the ocean, not a zoo," said Dad.

"Aquarium," muttered Charlie, still looking out to sea. "And anyway. She should be here. It's high tide."

"Maybe it's the weather?" suggested Mum.

"She's a dolphin," Charlie said sarcastically, turning around at last. "She lives in water. She's not gonna be scared of a drop of rain, is it? Do you think she's gonna look out the window and say, 'Ooh, I'm staying indoors. I haven't got an umbrella and a freaking jacket'?"

"All right, sorry, Mr. Grumpy," said Mum, her eyebrows raised. "No need to get angry."

"Well, don't be so dumb, then," he snapped.

"Whoa!" growled Dad. "Cut it out."

This was totally out of character for Charlie. The only times I'd ever seen him like this before was when he'd been frustrated he couldn't do something.

We sat there in awkward silence for another ten minutes, Charlie chucking more coins into the little telescope until he ran out of money. Eventually, with the rain soaking him to the bone, we peeled him away and dragged him back to the car.

On our way past a small office on the seafront, Charlie picked up a leaflet for a boat tour offering "incredible four-hour dolphin-watching tours around the coast" and handed it to Dad.

Dad rubbed the back of his neck, then tucked the leaflet into his pocket. "Well. Er. We'll see, eh, son?"

That evening, while the rest of us played a game of Clue, Charlie sat in the corner, drawing his dolphins and eating gummy bears. In fact, he hardly said two words all evening.

Later, in bed, he finally talked to me. "I wonder where she was," he said through the darkness. The dolphin was always a *she*. I guess because the old-timer had said so on Saturday.

"She'll probably show up tomorrow," I said.

"Maybe Dad'll take us on that boat trip?" said Charlie, his voice hopeful and excited. "They do 'em from the harbor. The old-timer said yesterday it's the best way to get up close to wildlife."

Dad had left the leaflet on the kitchen table. At twenty-five pounds for adults and fifteen for children, I seriously doubted we could afford it. "Wouldn't it be great if you had a pet dolphin in a tank?" I said, trying to change the subject. "You know, then you could see it every day."

The bedside light flicked on. Charlie doesn't wear his glasses or patch in bed, so his face always looks strange, but tonight he had an expression I'd never seen before—total disgust. "You really don't understand, do you?" he said. His voice was cold.

"Understand what?" I asked, confused.

But Charlie just grunted angrily and switched off the light. Then I heard him flop back to bed, his covers rustling as he turned away to face the wall.

I lay there, staring into the darkness. I had no idea what I'd said wrong.

Hiding and Escaping

I sit facing Charlie at a table. This train is great; all plush dark seats, clean carpets, and tinted windows. But I can't enjoy it because we've been sitting here for two minutes and we still haven't left the station. I can see Hen from my window wandering around on the platform, looking for us. After a while she pauses, confused. There's an awful pounding in my brain. I don't want to breathe. *Why isn't the train moving yet?*

The loudspeaker announces, *"We're sorry for the delay; we're waiting for a cargo train to pass through the station ahead of us, so sit back and relax and we'll be moving shortly."* The cheerfulness of the voice irritates me, like it's giving me good news. We *need* to get away from here before Hen sees us.

I grind my teeth together. On the platform, Hen is running her fingers through her blue hair. Then suddenly her head tilts to one side and she approaches our train, peering in through the next window to ours. Oh God. She's only ten feet away. Charlie and I duck under the table so we're hidden. *Why won't this train just get a move on?*

"This is really mean," I say. "After everything she's done for us. I shouldn't have listened to you."

"Bologna," says Charlie, his face flat against the wall. "We don't want her interfering with our business, do we? Other people are trouble. You think she cares about the dolphin? What if she makes us late?"

"You're the one jumping on a random train," I say, but Charlie just shrugs.

I peer over the table. Hen is moving along the platform away from us now. Part of me feels relieved, but this is still horrible. It's like someone's got hold of my guts in their fist and they're trying to rip them out. I suddenly find myself angry at Charlie. The way he's acting reminds me of our vacation when he didn't seem to care about anything else but the dolphin. While we were away, I sometimes wished he'd never seen it.

"You and your stupid dolphin," I hiss, surprised at how angry my voice sounds. I can't remember the last

time I got mad at him. An old woman across the aisle is staring at me, and Charlie's face is a mixture of shock and fear. I take a deep breath and lower my voice. "I'm sorry."

"Still not nice, though," he replies, and I know he's right. I'm only being like this because I feel bad about Hen. I huff out my cheeks and I'm about to say sorry again, but I don't because, for the second time that day, I've got that feeling of being watched. And when I turn to my right, there's Hen, glaring in at me through the window.

Emptiness

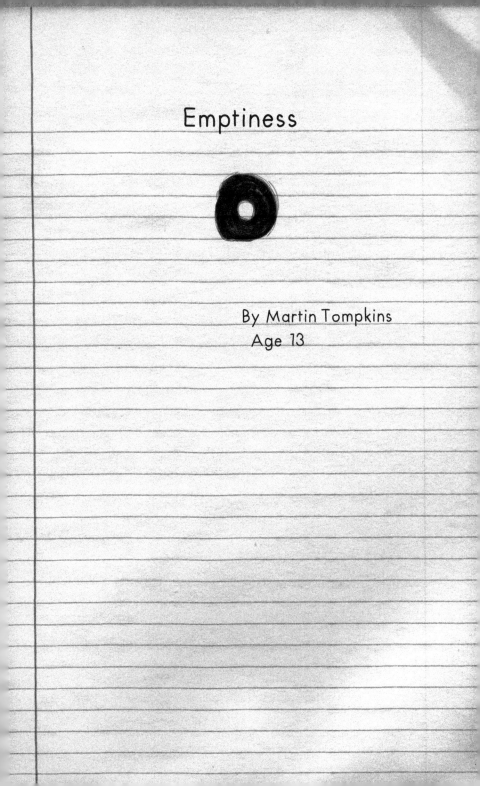

By Martin Tompkins
Age 13

Stage 5
(Adjusted and Clarified)

Plymouth to Par
(by luck, then by quick escape)

Distance—36 miles
Train

Hurt and Empty

I can't stand to catch Hen's eye. Behind the heavy makeup, she looks so *hurt*, so let down. "What are you *doing*?" she mouths at me, her forehead all creased around her eyebrow piercing.

I feel my mouth wobbling, trying to find words, but nothing comes out.

Hen slaps the window with both hands and storms away toward the door of the train. And now she's repeatedly jabbing the button. Luckily the door doesn't open.

When will this flipping train get out of here?

That stupid cheerful voice again: *"Ladies and gentlemen, we apologize again for the delay. Tea and coffee is available. . . ."*

I feel like screaming that I don't care about the tea and coffee. I just want to get away from here so that I won't feel so terrible anymore. But now Hen's back at the window.

"Sorry," I mouth at her, but she's already turned her back and she's prowling off down the platform.

I sit back in the seat, head in my hands. There's part of me that's surprised I'm not having another meltdown. I guess that maybe the one in the alleyway was like taking the lid off of a shaken-up bottle of Coke. Everything fizzed out, and there's nothing left now.

"Good riddance," says Charlie, dusting his palms together, and it takes everything in my body not to whack him.

Fuming silently, I grab the notebook and pen from my bag and try to come up with a poem. But I can't write anything beyond the title, so I start drawing a dot on the page. Then I make it bigger, pressing harder and harder until the tip breaks through the paper and you can see the lines on the page below. The poem was going to be called "Emptiness," because that's how I'm feeling right now. Mr. Hendrix would probably look at the dot and the hole and say, "Great job. That looks like a pretty good picture of emptiness to me." But this isn't really a consolation.

I feel so stupid. All I can think of is how this was such a terrible idea. The entire trip. I should've known Charlie would act like this. I wanted it to be magical. I wanted him to enjoy it. But something about that dolphin just makes him so single-minded and unpredictable.

Rescue

The next day, when I woke up for breakfast, Charlie was already checking Dolphinwatch on Dad's phone.

"There's something wrong," he said, before I'd even had a chance to say good morning. "She's still not been back."

"It's eight in the morning," I yawned. "Give her a chance."

But Charlie kept tapping the screen to update it, which was totally pointless.

Dad strolled in and clapped his hands together. "Right, boys! Get dressed. We're going to be out all day. Big surprise."

"We're going on a boat trip?" asked Charlie, bouncing up and down.

"Definitely not," said Dad. "I've had enough of staring out to sea to last a lifetime."

Charlie dumped the phone onto the sofa and screwed up his face like a baby. "Aw."

Dad ignored him. "Nope. We're going to the zoo!"

"Cool!" I said. I love the zoo.

"But what about the dolphin?" cried Charlie, "It's not been back to the harbor, and if we went out on a boat, then—"

"We weighed up the cost of the boat trip, love," said Mum kindly, "and it was just too expensive. We got an online discount for the zoo. They've even got a penguin pool. It'll be just the same."

This was the wrong thing to say.

"No. It. Won't!" cried Charlie, stamping his feet. "And what about high tide? We'll miss it. It's this afternoon at th—"

"Look, son," said Dad, mildly irritated, "I've already bought the tickets and we're not spending another minute at that harbor."

"We'll go tomorrow morning, Charlie," said Mum, appearing at Dad's shoulder. "Before we go home. Promise."

"But . . ." said Dad.

Mum squeezed his arm and gave him a look that said *don't argue*. Dad sighed.

So off we went to Newquay zoo. It took ages to get there because of the traffic, and it seemed like even longer because Charlie was sulking all the way. Then, just as we arrived, Dad got a text from his service provider asking him if he'd meant to go three times over his internet limit this week and how his next bill would be over fifty pounds, so that made *two* grumpy people.

Personally, I thought the zoo was great. We saw lions, monkeys, red pandas, lemurs, and loads of other animals. Charlie wasn't quite as impressed. He dragged his feet all day, moaning about how pathetic it was. He didn't even smile when Mum took a photo of me and Dad standing in front of a sign that said "Warty Pigs" without us realizing. The whole day Charlie was a massive, glowering cloud hanging over our fun.

As we got in the car to drive back to the cottage, Mum said, "Well that was amazing!"

"Incredible," said Dad, who'd eventually got over his cell-phone bill.

"Not *real* nature, though, is it?" said Charlie. "It's just a big, cruel animal prison."

Weird Relief

Finally, the train roars to life and we ease our way out of the station. I still feel awful about Hen, but now that we're finally moving, there's also a kind of weird relief in the back of my mind. Charlie and I are on the move again, wherever it is we're going.

I even feel ready to write some poems again. I quickly jot one down about how happy I was to see Charlie again on the platform at Plymouth. It only takes about a minute because the pen just dances across the page. Afterward, I also write down the chant I had in my head back in the alleyway in Exeter. It seems important to do this, even though I'd rather forget all about my panic attack.

As I finish the poems and put my notebook away, Charlie is back to being excited again. "Right, well, that's that. Can we have a cookie from that tin now? I'm starving."

How many times . . . ? I think. I hand him the other half of my ham-and-jam sandwich from this morning and look out of the window as we leave the town behind, crossing a muddle of tracks past rusted-out old engines and dilapidated carriages until the train eventually runs straight.

"Ladies and gentlemen, welcome to the delayed fifteen-twelve service to Penzance, calling at . . ." says the cheerful loudspeaker voice. I sit upright and listen as it trawls through the names of towns until it comes to: *". . . Hayle. St. Erth."*

"That's it!" I say, snapping my fingers. "St. Erth. That's our stop. I remember it now. That's where we've got to change trains for St. Bernards."

"So that means we're on the right train?" says Charlie. "And we're gonna make it?"

"Yep," I reply, drumming my hands on the table. "Ha-ha! Good news at last."

This is a pretty amazing coincidence. Of all the trains we could've randomly gotten on, we chose the right one. At least things are working out for us, even if . . .

There's a bit of a pause when neither of us says anything.

"You could look happier about it," says Charlie.

I don't reply.

Charlie leans toward me. "You're not still thinking about that *girl*, are you?"

"Shut up. . . ." I say, wafting my hand in his direction.

"Look," he says, "this is our trip, right? Just me and you. Epic vacation replay. We don't want some girl we don't even know weasling her way in on it, do we?"

"I guess not," I say reluctantly.

"And anyway, if I hadn't dragged you onto this train, then it might've been ages till the next one. We might not have made it in time."

I'm about to tell him that okay, maybe he's right when I see the conductor come into our carriage. "Get down!" I whisper. Charlie ducks under the table, then crawls under my seat and wriggles out of sight. Sometimes being so tiny has its advantages.

When the conductor reaches us, she asks to see my ticket, so I show her. I feel quite in control until Charlie starts tickling behind my knees.

I giggle out loud, and the conductor raises an eyebrow. "You all right?" she asks. She's pretty young, maybe late twenties. A little bit overweight. Pants pulled high up over her stomach.

Biting my lip, I kick Charlie with my heel, and he stops.

The conductor studies my ticket and narrows her eyes. "Preston to St. Bernards, huh? Can I . . . ah . . . ask what your name is?"

This is a totally unexpected question. I feel my heart jump. Why does she want to know?

"I . . . my name?" I stammer. My mouth is seriously dry and my brain is blank.

"Don't tell her," whispers Charlie from under the seat. I muffle his voice by coughing and stamping my foot. The conductor tilts her head to one side suspiciously. Blood is pumping in my ears. I need to come up with something quick.

"Wesley . . ." I say, unsure of where this is going. "Er. Wesley Lizard."

Why did I say that?

"Wesley . . . *Lizard*?" asks the conductor.

"Yes. It's. Er. Italian," I say, sounding more and more ridiculous with every word. "My dad was from Italy. He was big in spaghetti."

Spaghetti?! This is awful.

There's a horrible pause while the conductor taps my ticket with her pencil. Then, sounding unconvinced, she says, "O-*kay*. Careful on your travels." She hands me my ticket, then moves away.

As soon as she's gone, Charlie pokes his head up between my knees. "*Ciao*, Wesley," he says in this ridiculous Italian accent. "Make-a me some spaghetti or I break-a your face."

I look at him for a moment. *Wesley Lizard.* What was I thinking? I can't believe she bought it! Before I know it, my shoulders are shaking and my eyes are scrunched up with laughter and I can barely breathe. Then Charlie's face turns serious and he says, "Uh-oh," and disappears under the seat again. I look up and stop laughing immediately.

Hen is standing over me. And her face is like thunder. "What the hell are you doing?" she snarls, sitting down angrily in the seat next to me and dumping her backpack on the table.

Questions and Escapes

I don't say anything to her. I don't know what I *can* say. I was kind of hoping Charlie would help me out, but by the time Hen sits down, he's slid away under the seats. He'll be miles away in no time; he's like a worm.

I'm on my own again.

"That was a really crappy thing to do," she snaps. "Leaving me behind after all I've done for you."

I want to explain, but all I can manage is a whispered "It was Charlie. He—"

"Your brother?" she says, looking around. "And where is he now, then?"

I glance around just in time to see the toilet door at the end of the train car closing. Sure enough, a moment later the occupied sign lights up to show that the bathroom is in use. *Thanks a bunch,* I think.

"I had to beg them to let me on," she continues, her voice all angry and teacherish. "Told the guard on the platform that you've got a terminal illness and I've got your medication."

"Sorry," I croak. I realize that I'm hugging my backpack so tightly that the cookie tin is digging into my ribs.

"You're *sorry*? Oh, well, that's okay, then," she scoffs, running her hand through her blue hair. "Wish I'd never bothered."

Without saying anything, I take off her coat and push it toward her. I hadn't noticed how warm I was until now. "Here," I say.

"Unbelievable. I don't care about the stupid coat. I care about . . ." Her voice trails away and she starts again. "The one time I meet someone who . . ."

Again her voice trails away. She breathes in and out a few times. Then she slaps the table and says, "Look. Forget it. You and your brother have your stupid vacation. Sorry for helping."

With that, she snatches the coat from me, shoulders her bag, and stomps off along the train, sitting down a few rows away on the other side of the aisle. My stomach feels like lead.

The train rattles on and on, past fields and straggly towns with the sea beyond. After a while, Charlie comes back and dumps himself into his old seat again.

"No, you can't have a cookie," I say wearily.

"What did *she* want?"

I shake my head. "She's mad because I ran off."

Charlie leans in. "We're so much better off without her. Seriously. Look at her hair. I think she might be an alien."

"An *alien*?"

"Yeah. I saw a show about them. She probably wants to eat your brain. Anyway, I told you. This is *our* trip, so she can get lost."

"Shh," I say, but it's obvious when I look over that Hen can hear every word. She's facing away from us, but she's shaking her head and her knuckles are white on the armrest in front.

"No," says Charlie loudly. "She needs to leave us alone."

At that point, Hen suddenly stands up. As she's turning around, Charlie runs back to the bathroom again. I feel my body go tense as she marches toward me. Luckily she's blocked off by the conductor, who's appeared from nowhere and is standing over my shoulder.

"Ah, hello again, *Wesley*." The conductor smiles, bending forward. Hen stands seething in the aisle next to her, waiting for her chance.

"Hi," I say, trying to ignore Hen and concentrate on the conductor.

The conductor clears her throat awkwardly. "I've . . . ah . . . called the police and . . . ah . . . do you have any ID?"

"ID?" I say. "What do you . . . ?"

"All the staff on this line have been asked to look out for a boy traveling from Preston to St. Bernards. Martin . . . ah . . . Tompkins. Police thought it sounded like a bit of a coincidence when I told them about you."

The train sways like it's slowing down, and I feel nauseous.

"They told me to double-check before we reach the next stop."

I make a strange squeaking sound.

"So," she continues, "if you could just confirm your name?"

I look around for Charlie. He's out of the bathroom again, lingering in the aisle, and he looks back at me, shaking his head. My throat is beginning to tighten. "I'm . . ."

"Wesley!" exclaims Hen from behind the conductor. "There you are!"

I turn to her, eyes wide open.

"My brother's such a little ragamuffin," she chuckles as she squeezes past the conductor and puts her body between us. "He's always running off like this. Come on, this is our stop."

The conductor looks confused. "He's your brother. So you're his . . ."

"Sister, yes. That's how it usually works," says Hen, like she's dealing with a complete imbecile. "We're the Lizards. Funny name. Dad was Egyptian."

"*He* said Italian," says the conductor, confused.

The train brakes hard into the station. The conductor staggers a few steps and collides with Hen.

"Oops, careful," says Hen pleasantly. "Dad was both. Moved out from Egypt to Italy to build pyramids. Anyway. Lovely talking with you, but we have to go."

I have no idea where we are.

"Come on, *Wes*," says Hen, pulling me to my feet. Her hand is digging into mine a little bit too hard as she turns to the conductor with a sweet smile. "Good luck finding this other kid."

With that, she practically drags me off the train, with Charlie trailing behind us. We don't look back. On the next platform, there's another, smaller train waiting to leave and, without checking where it's going, she pulls me onto it just before its doors close.

Stage 6

Par to Newquay

21 miles (in the wrong direction)
Train

Questions and Surfboards

The train is pretty packed. Every other person here seems to be a fluffy, blond-haired dude in shorts, or a girl with denim cutoffs and a messy ponytail. We don't even bother to look for somewhere to sit because the only spare seats have bags or surfboards propped up on them. So we just stand in between the two clattering cars along with more bulky luggage.

"Where are we going?" I ask Hen. I'm wearing the backpack, and I can feel the sharp, comforting corners of the cookie tin on my back.

"Away from the people who want to find *you*. Now don't move. I'm going in here," she commands, and she shoves her backpack down at my feet and disappears into the bathroom.

"This is the 4:15 service to Newquay," says a bored, nasal voice down a loudspeaker. A bunch of surfer dudes down the car cheer at the mention of Newquay.

"Calling at . . ."

"Aw! I hate Newquay!" whines Charlie. "I thought we were going to St. Bernards. What about the dolphin?"

I try to ignore him as he stamps his foot and moans on and on about the zoo and the dolphin.

Newquay. Right. Well, that explains the surfers. Everyone knows Newquay's where people go to surf. And I know from our zoo trip that it's not too far from St. Bernards, so at least we're going in something like the right direction.

"Look," I say as patiently as possible, "we'll be able to change trains and get back to St. Bernards in time for high tide. I'm sure of it. It could be much worse. We could've been caught by that conductor, eh?"

Charlie shakes his head. "If we miss the dolphin because of her . . ."

I smile nervously, my stomach in knots.

For a moment, I'm surprised that *I'm* feeling nervous, because I realize I'm not just nervous for him but for me as well. But then I realize something that I've probably known deep down all along; that this trip isn't only about him. It's about me too. *We* both need to see the dolphin again. It feels like I've stepped into a room I'd kept locked from myself. Of course I'm doing it for me as well as for Charlie. We've got to get there. This is our journey. Our dolphin.

I've tried not to think about the last time I saw it, but the memory of it suddenly bubbles up in my mind and for the first time, I don't push it back down. It's a weird kind of flashback when I replay it, not like any of my other memories. It's not clear like a film, or misty like a dream. It's jagged. Cracked. Like I'm watching it through a shattered window.

Nets and Swimming

The last morning of the vacation. Sunny. Hot, even at seven o'clock. Charlie had got us all out of bed by six. Car stuffed full again, packing was more rushed this time, so there are bags on our knees in the back. We put the cottage keys through the mailbox at reception, then started driving to St. Bernards in silence. Nice and early, so no problems getting a parking space. The bay is perfect. Tide in. Water emerald-clear, waves gently slapping the sea wall. Boats nodding up and down. Mum saying she'd miss this. A handful of tourists walking along the front. Charlie running straight to the fence, clambering up it and staring out nervously. Biting his lip. Old-timer strolling along. Saying hello but Charlie too nervous to reply. Me realizing suddenly what this dolphin meant to Charlie and why he hated the zoo so much. The dolphin is freedom. Life. The ability to *do*. To live, in the way that Charlie never can. *Don't get too excited. Don't go running off. Make sure you've got your inhaler. You're sick again, so you'll have to miss out on that. Why can't you concentrate? Sit at the table with the other airheads.*

And right then I want to hug him. Tell him I love him.

But I don't. Because at that moment the dolphin swims into the harbor. It's Dad who sees it. A black fin. A patch of shade moving slowly among the boats. Charlie yelling. Relief. Happiness. Dolphin rounds the boats and moves into the space ahead of us. Then we see. The tired, labored swimming. The hoarse, painful cloud of vapor coming out of the blowhole. The tangled orange fishing net trailing from its tail. The vivid scarlet stripe of flesh above its fluke where the net has slashed the skin.

Does it look right at us, or do I imagine that?

All of us concentrating on it too much to notice Charlie slip between the railings. The scuffle of his feet on the ground makes us turn. Desperate shouts from Mum uselessly in her throat as he plunges, limbs windmilling, ten feet through the air. Awful splash when he hits the water. Flailing arms fighting toward the dolphin. *He can't swim! He can't swim!* Slow progress. Wave lapping over him. Spluttering. Then another wave. Charlie under the water. Dad leaping in behind him. Charlie's outline fading as he sinks. Dad ducking down. Grabbing for him. Up for air. Back again. Old-timer going in after him. Diving gracefully. Perfect landing. Surfacing. Deep breath. The pair of them down one more time. This time Charlie pulled up by his ankle. Dad and Old-Timer clutching at a life jacket someone's thrown over. Kicking violently with Charlie dragged floppy doll behind them to the harbor steps. Dad's face hideous with panic. Mum screaming. Howling. Not a human sound. Someone meeting Dad on the steps to help him up. Charlie's body hauled onto the pavement. Face gray. Eyes glassy. Looking at me but not seeing. My hollowed-out insides. Dad pumping his heart. Old-Timer blowing into his mouth. Mum shaking his arm. Again. Again. Again.

Nothing.

Awful silence.

More blowing. More pumping.

Then a splutter.

Water bursting out of Charlie's mouth like a volcano.

Retching.

Body convulsing.

Onto his side.

Violently sick.

Painful, rasping breaths.

Gulping down air.

Mum clutching him.

Charlie.

Escape and Demands

The longer we stand between the cars, the more agitated Charlie gets. He's bouncing up and down nervously, and his eyes keep flicking toward the locked bathroom door. "We've gotta get away from her," he says, nibbling his thumb. "Why can't you see it? She'll ruin everything."

"Where can we go?" I say.

His face twitches and he blinks hard behind his specs. "This was meant to be *our* trip, you know. Me and you. I told you that she'd make us late. Now she's dragging us off somewhere stupid. What if—"

"Stop it!" I say. A couple of surf dudes sitting on the floor look up at me. One tells me to *chill*, so I turn my back on them and lower my voice to Charlie. "I promise we'll see the dolphin tonight, whatever happens. Okay?"

I know this is a stupid thing to promise. The ocean isn't an aquarium, like the old man said, right? But I'm desperate. I can't have Charlie running off again.

He knows it's a stupid promise too. "I'm going over there," he sighs, and he picks his way down the aisle, fist-bumping the surfer dudes on his way past and saying stuff like, "Hey, bro, way to ride the gnarly tubes," and "Let's get in motion with the ocean," in this ridiculous, gravelly American accent. Even when he's in a bad mood, he can't resist being crazy.

I watch as he sits himself down uninvited on the only free seat in the car. It's about halfway down, with his back to me, next to a couple of men with dreadlocks and silly pants who look like they're asleep. Just as he sits down, the toilet door opens and Hen steps out.

"Well, good job for not running off," she says sarcastically.

I don't reply. She stares at me for a few moments. "So, are you going to tell me what all this is about?"

I shrug. "What do you mean?"

She scratches her head. "Er . . . dunno. Maybe like

why are you running away? *Why* are you going to St. Bernards? And *why* are the police and a whole bunch of people who work on trains trying to catch you?"

I'm looking at my shoes, moving imaginary dirt around on the floor. "Like I said. I'm taking my brother to see a dolphin."

Hen doesn't say anything, and when I look up at her, she's staring at me really hard. Finally she takes a deep breath. When she speaks this time, her voice is softer. "I'm *trying* to help you, Martin. I saw you back there in Exeter and you were . . ." She sighs, looking for the right words. "You *scared* me. I couldn't just leave you there like that."

My face screws up. I don't want to think about what happened in the alley.

"Look," she says, "just tell me the truth. You can trust me. I read your poem, remember. We're similar, you and me. Our brains work the same way. That's why I had to help. It's your parents, isn't it? You never answered me back in the alley. But it's always parents. That's why *my* head's all over the place. I've been through it all, remember. I haven't seen my dad since I was a kid, and as for my mum? Well, let's just say she doesn't approve of anything I do *ever*."

"I don't know what you're talking about," I whisper, but it's like someone else is speaking. "We're just re-creating our vacation, that's all."

"Hang on," she says, "where's your brother?"

Eyes toward the floor, I point down the train car to where he's sitting. Immediately there's a hand under my chin and she's holding my face so I have to look at her.

"Down there. I told you," I protest, tears prickling behind my eyes, a basketball-size lump in my throat.

She lets go, and we stare at each other for what seems like ages. And then her face changes like she's just realized something.

There's a warm pain where her hand was and I'm trying to focus on it because the rest of my body feels like a balloon that's floating through a room of sharp nails, ready to burst at any moment, and I can't breathe without my chest shaking and creaking and she's still staring and maybe Charlie will lend me his inhaler if I ask him and then Hen is speaking and it takes me a few moments to realize what she's saying and when the words finally register they just squeeze the breath out of my body and I suddenly know what it feels like to ride a wave like these surfers then have the whole weight of the ocean just crash down on you and my legs give way and my back slides down the wall and I'm sitting on the floor.

Time ticks by.

I've covered my eyes with my arms. The rattling of the train is unbearably loud, but it isn't loud enough to block out what she says to me next. I can't get away from the words she said. Even minutes later, they echo through me, ricocheting around my skull and slicing through my brain like machine-gun bullets.

"I didn't even think about it at the time, 'cause I was so mad at you and we were in such a rush," she'd said to me, "but nobody got on this train with us. And nobody was on the last train with you either. You're on your own."

Stage 7

A Bench on Newquay Train Station
to a Bench on Newquay Train Station

0 Miles
Sitting Down

The End of the Line

We've been at Newquay for a while. I'm on a cold metal bench right at the end of the platform, as far away as I can be from the main part of the station. The surf dudes all poured out of here ages ago, shouldering their bags and surfboards and disappearing into the town. There's a faint salty, seaside tang in the air.

The station clock clicks through seven minutes past five. A few people wander around here and there, waiting for trains, but the station seems desolate. Guards are laughing together down the other end of the platform. An old geezer shuffles up and down to kill time. My eyes follow a single plastic bag as it dances past in the wind. It somersaults along the track, then gets tangled on the buffers. This is the end of the line.

Hen returns. Sits down next to me. A hot drink in a paper cup is pushed into my hands. "Here. Drink this. Tea with three sugars."

I sip it. Too hot.

Hen puts her arm around me. Her body is warm but not soft. "You're freezing," she says. I clutch the tea toward my chest and hunch my shoulders. I should really get my jacket out of the backpack. The clock ticks on through the seconds and minutes. A stationary train on the other platform coughs into life. Lights flicker on inside it. The old geezer walks around to it and climbs on. The plastic bag is stuck on the buffer, flapping uselessly in the breeze.

"Look," she says. Deep breath. "I'm sorry. For . . ."

Her voice drifts off. I sip the tea again. Still too hot.

"It's fine," I say, my voice dry like sandpaper. And then, without looking at her, I start to speak.

I tell her about Charlie. About the vacation. About how he dived in to save the dolphin's life.

"Oh God," she says, hand over her mouth.

I nod. Then I continue the story.

Going Home

Someone had called an ambulance. They wrapped Charlie up in blankets and this tinfoil stuff, then raced off to the nearest hospital, with Mum in the back and me and Dad following behind in the car. The drive to Truro seemed to take forever, even though it was only about a half hour.

At the hospital, Mum went in with Charlie, while I sat in a waiting room watching Dad pace up and down. He was wearing someone else's clothes. A woman had come out of her house and given him her husband's sweater and jeans. They were both about three sizes too small. At any other time, we'd have made a joke about it.

Finally, sometime in the afternoon, we were allowed to go in and see Charlie. He was propped up in bed looking pale and weak, and holding a gray cardboard bowl in his hands. There were these electric pads wired up to his chest, and beeping machines behind him. It reminded me of that photo of him from when he was born. "How's it going, bum face?" I said, trying not to cry.

"Great news"—he grinned—"I've been picked for the Olympic swimming team. One of the coaches saw me. I'm doing the fifty-meters vertical sink."

We all had a little chuckle at that, because it kind of broke the tension a bit, but then Charlie's laugh sort of morphed into this coughing fit. They were really horrible, wet coughs. Spluttering. Bubbling. His heart monitor started beeping wildly. Mum jabbed at the panic button, and in two seconds, a nurse and doctor flew through the doors and pulled him upright in bed and smacked his back; then he spewed up all this water into his cardboard bowl. Slowly he caught his breath and everything settled down again.

"Sorry about that," said Charlie, wiping the spit away from his mouth. "Where are my manners?"

I gave a weak smile.

"To be on the safe side, we'll keep him here for a while so we can keep an eye on him," said the doctor, listening to Charlie breathing through her stethoscope. "Especially with his medical history."

"I'm all right," said Charlie, but the doctor ignored him.

"Oh, and while I remember," said the nurse, "someone calling himself the *old-timer* rang. Apparently the dolphin is fine. Some fishermen managed to cut the net off it."

Charlie gave an enormous grin.

"You're a real hero," I said. And I believed it too.

Cold Tea

"Oh, Martin," says Hen. One hand is still over her mouth. The other has kind of snaked its way around my shoulders. "You must've been so relieved."

I swirl my tea around the paper cup, then take a gulp. It's cold and disgustingly sweet. I feel like I've been talking for ages.

I know she's looking at me, waiting for me to answer. Slowly I turn my eyes to meet hers. And there's a split second when I can tell she's reading something from my face. But I don't want her to read it, so I turn away again and suddenly fling the cup as far as I can. It flips over and over, tea flying out of it like brown sparks from a firework. The cup bounces across the tracks, and my shoulders crumple. My head flops into my hands. Her fingers dig into my shoulders.

"What's wrong?" she says, but her voice is distant.

My breath seems to come in ragged bursts that tear

at my chest and arms. And the words are welling up inside me, forcing their way to the surface like dolphins kicking themselves up, until finally they burst out of my mouth and I start to speak again.

The Curtains

It was almost a week later when it happened. He'd been fine leaving the hospital. On fire in fact. He'd only been there two nights, but the nurses all came out to see him off. They thought he was amazing. *Brightened up our lives,* they said. *Wish they were all like him. Breath of fresh air.*

We'd driven the seven hours all the way home and got back to the house in the evening. Then, in the middle of the night, Charlie had pains in his chest. Rushed straight to the emergency room. Checkup. Night in for observation. But by the morning everything was back to normal. *You've had a big shock. Take it easy. Rest. Come straight back if you notice anything out of the ordinary. Always best to take precautions.*

He was quiet for the rest of the week, sitting on the sofa wearing his pj's and watching back-to-back *Peppa Pig*s on TV, eating his ham-and-jam sandwiches and drawing pictures of dolphins in his little pad. He even joked about how sick kids get to swim with dolphins and maybe he'd be allowed to do it now.

And then it happened. Nothing dramatic. No fanfares. It just happened.

Thursday morning. I opened the curtains in our room like I always do to wake him up.

And that was it.

He was gone.

I knew it instantly. Cold. Gray. Still. But peaceful. Eyes closed. And on the floor by the side of his bed was his pad. He must've been drawing before he went to sleep. On the open page there was a picture of a leaping dolphin. "To Martin," it said underneath. "From Charlie."

Shadows

The plastic bag on the buffers has given up trying to escape. It's dangling limp and still. The train on the other platform eases out of the station.

"Oh, Martin," she says.

I shrug, picking at my thumbnails. I'm surprised that I want to talk about what happened. It's the first time I have. Not that anybody else wants to. Mum and Dad never talk about it. People at school avoid it like a massive unexploded mine.

Eventually I carry on. "You know what? No one was even sure exactly what caused it. I mean, his heart *was* terrible. Always had been. The doctors think it was probably something to do with the shock of going in the water. But maybe it was always going to happen. Maybe it was a bit of both."

"Oh, Martin," Hen whispers again.

"He's with me all the time, you know," I say. Hen squeezes me tighter, and I realize there are tears running down her cheeks that mix with mine as our faces touch. "Real as if he was sitting here. I talk to him and he talks back."

"Like an imaginary friend?" she says. Immediately I think she feels embarrassed to have said this, like it's insensitive or something. But I know what she means.

"No," I reply. "More than that. He's a part of me. He's in everything I do. Everything I say. Everything I *think*."

There's a pause. "Is that who you were arguing with on the train before? I thought you'd gone . . ."

Her voice trails off. She doesn't want to say *crazy*. I understand. "I'm sorry about running off," I say. "He made me do it. I mean, *I* made me do it. I was scared and . . . the part of me that's Charlie didn't want you to find out about everything. It's hard to explain."

Hen squeezes me tighter. "You don't have to."

"Sometimes I can almost touch him," I say after a long time. "I even fell onto my butt at Preston station 'cause I was picturing him tripping over me. He's always there."

"That's so *sweet*, you know?"

I shake my head. "Not now it isn't. I need to let him go."

"Don't say that."

"Not forget about him. I need to just, you know, let him rest. We all do. It's been fourteen months. We've got to live." I can feel my voice getting stronger and louder. "That's all Charlie wanted. To be alive. Like the dolphin. Mum, she can't even get out of bed. Dad, he's never at home, he just works all the time. Me—I keep having these panic attacks. None of us ever even *talk* about Charlie. I want my family back."

I can feel that my hands have made fists, and I'm pounding my knees as I speak. "You know what? He was cremated, and Mum wouldn't let anyone bury his ashes. We couldn't even say goodbye to him. That's why I've got to go to St. Bernards. I *know* that if I go back . . ."

"You'll be able to say goodbye," says Hen, wiping her nose on the sleeve of her multi-colored coat. "So when do you need to be in St. Bernards?"

"Seven," I say. We both look at the clock. Five twenty.

"I'll get you there," she says, standing up. "Stay here. I'll ask someone."

Almost There . . . But Not Quite

A spider crawled up
The inside of a glass.
It took him all day.
Slithering, sliding on the slippery glass-cliff face,
Sticky liquid weighing him down
Clogging the tiny hairs on his legs.
He fought and strained,
Desperate to escape.
Three steps forward.
Two steps back.
Until finally he reached the top.
Exhausted, he rested on the lip of the glass.
Then someone took a drink
And swallowed him.

By Martin Tompkins
Age 13

Stage 8

Newquay Station to a Pub, Then Back Again

About a mile
Walking There, Sprinting Back

Disappointments and Solutions

I decide to write a poem. I hadn't realized it till now, but I'm at the second-to-last page in the book. I'm about to start, my pen hovering over the page, when Hen comes back. Her face doesn't look good. "Bit of a problem," she says.

She's right.

It turns out we *can* get to St. Bernards, but it'll take almost three hours. I don't understand this. I check on my mileage chart and it's only thirty-odd miles away, but Hen says that the trains are terrible around here and you've always got to change somewhere to get somewhere else.

"So we won't get there until eight? But we'll miss high tide," says Charlie. His voice is suddenly quieter, more distant, like he's on the other side of a window. I turn to look for him like I always do, but he's not there. Not to look at anyway. For a moment, I panic, searching all around me. I can't be without him. But then I begin to understand. It's like talking about him has shifted something.

"This is hopeless," says Charlie, muffled. And I imagine, but can't see, how he might flop down on the bench with his hands under his chin. "I feel like a spider stuck in a glass."

He's right. I can't see him but he's right. This is desperate.

Hen is talking to me. Charlie's voice is babbling on. I know this might not be the time, but before I can do anything about it, the pen is scratching rapidly across the page. I'm writing another poem, about Charlie's spider. I start to feel better, even though the poem's basically about how hopeless everything is.

Writing is how I've managed to cope with everything since last year. It's the only way I know to get my thoughts out. When I finally came back to school, three weeks after the start of the new year, I was kind of drifting around like a ghost in the hallways and classrooms. Then one day my English teacher, Mr. Hendrix, called me in to see him. He said he'd had an idea: a poetry club with one member—*me*. At first I thought it was stupid, but he told me that I could turn up at his office whenever I wanted, whether he was there or not. He'd even squared it away with my teachers. If I needed to just wander out of class, I could. As long as I was writing he didn't mind. He even gave me a green notebook. I asked if I could decorate it, and he said *Sure thing, daddy-o*, which is one of his little phrases. I stuck Charlie's last picture he ever drew on the front of it, then wrapped it with plastic to protect it.

Without the poetry, without Mr. Hendrix, I wouldn't have gotten through the year.

I know that Hen is watching me write. I can feel her wanting to say something, but she waits until I've finished and the notebook is back in my backpack.

"Better?" she says.

I nod. She just seems to understand.

"How much money have you got?"

I count it out. Between us we've got eighteen pounds. With her holding my hand, we stride through the station and out into the town. People are buzzing about everywhere, out for the evening I guess. I stand close to

Hen as she argues the price with a taxi driver.

"No, no," he says, "fifty pounds to St. Bernards an' that's the best you'll get on a Sat'day, love."

I can tell she wants to fight or yell, but she knows this won't do any good. She looks around nervously, then shouts over to some guys who are passing by. Tight T-shirts. Bulging muscles. Gelled hair.

"Where's the busiest pub around here?" she says.

"We haven't got time for you to have a drink," I say, but Hen ignores me.

The guys all make sounds and say crude things. Hen rolls her eyes. "In your dreams, boys. Just tell me."

They just walk off laughing. An older man and his wife must've overheard. He gives us directions through town and tells us to have a great night, and he hopes I've got some ID on me 'cause I don't look a day over fourteen, if he's honest.

I wince.

"Right. Let's go," says Hen.

"Where?" I say.

Hen smiles. "Pub of course. We gotta earn you enough for a taxi, old boy."

Flames

We find the pub no problem. It's a great big place. Music thumping out of it. Football on big screens inside. Tons of people even though it's still early; musclemen, surfers, really lovely-looking girls in short skirts, all laughing and drinking inside, and pouring out onto the wooden deck that overlooks the road. It makes me feel really out of place and nervous, but Hen squeezes my shoulder and tells me everything's going to be fine.

It takes Hen about three seconds to get ready. Backpack off her shoulders. Coat off. Clubs, sticks, and paraffin out onto the pavement. Floppy hat thrust into my hand.

"You got any food?" she asks before she starts. "I'm starving."

I don't want to tell her about the *special-leftover-from-Christmas* cookies. They're for St.

Bernards. I said I'd save them and I will. But I've got the ham-and-jam sandwich I made for Charlie still in my backpack. I really did make the sandwich for him, but of course he wasn't here to eat it. She eyes it uneasily, but once she's had a bite, she tells me it's actually delicious and she shovels the rest down in no time.

Then she begins.

Doctor Lizard was right. She is *incredible*. Without any introduction, she just starts. She begins by flinging the clubs in the air, four of them spinning, crossing them over, catching them backhand, forehand, behind the back, arcing throws that loop high into the air, hands placed perfectly to catch. Eyes closed then open again. A growing sense of realization and appreciation from the pub. People nudging each other and turning around. Others pressing from inside to see. Then she catches three clubs before bending forward and catching the other one on the back of her neck. Massive applause. A bow.

Then out come the sticks and she pours some paraffin onto them before slipping the little bottle into her back pocket. The crowd says *oooh*.

"Who's got a lighter?" she calls out. I know already that she's got one, but this must be part of the act. A big guy comes out and holds one up for her. His friends cheer. He lights the first stick with a *woof.*

"Stay here. You're perfect," she says, lighting the other three sticks off the first one. "Stand up straight. Hold these. Don't move. I don't want you to die."

She's speaking to him, but really she's talking to the audience. The big guy's friends laugh loud and hard but he does what she says, holding the sticks out wide as the flames dance up into the air. Then she climbs up him like a ladder and sits on his shoulders before taking the sticks off him in one hand.

"Hold this leg and this hand," she says firmly, offering him her free hand. The flaming sticks are held as far away as possible in the other.

Big Guy looks surprised. Worried. The crowd goes tense. And in a few seconds she's crouching on his shoulders. Bit of a wobble. Then she's standing up slowly and letting go of his hand. Big Guy's trying not to look like he's straining as he grips her ankles. A small cheer. And Hen starts to juggle. Four flaming sticks dancing through the sky. Then she catches all of them and produces the bottle from her back pocket. A quick gulp and a hard blow on the sticks. A ball of flame erupts through the air. There's an enormous cheer; then she leaps off Big Guy's shoulders, lands on the ground, and bows.

"Go around with the hat. *Quick*," she hisses, pushing me toward the terrace as the crowd goes wild. She puts the torches out on her tongue and holds up Big Guy's arm. He gives her a kiss on her cheek. And meanwhile I'm on the patio, edging between bodies, tables, chairs. Money rains into the hat *ching-ching-ching*. Big Guy's friend even drops in a tenner and the hat's getting heavier till Hen yells, "Martin. Go. Police."

And the people part to let me through and we're sprinting through the streets, laughing our heads off, the hat clutched to my chest. All I can think about is one thing; Charlie would LOVE this.

Stage 9

Newquay to St. Bernards

31 miles
Taxi

Quiet and Cookies

The taxi swings through the suburbs of Newquay, and soon we're out onto the main road. It's dusk now, and the other cars are putting on their lights. The euphoria of the juggling and the money didn't last long. Back at the station, it was time for business. Huddled on a bench, we counted the money—sixty-two pounds including what we already had. *Not bad,* said Hen. She asked if I wanted some grub or anything but I said no and we were straight into the first cab in the line, price agreed and off we went.

Now here we are. I feel nervous and a bit subdued. I haven't said anything in the ten minutes since we climbed inside. To keep myself going, I've looked at my mileage chart and added up all the distance we'll have traveled today. It should've been three hundred and seventy but it'll be more like four hundred and twenty-one by the time we get there, if I count all the walking and running as well.

My backpack is on the seat next to me, with Hen on the other side. She squeezes my hand over the top of it and smiles to me. The clock in the cab blinks six twenty.

"How long will it take?" I say.

The taxi driver rubs his neck. "Hard to say that, boy. 'Nother forty-five minutes, give or take?"

I bite my lip.

Hen's got her phone in her hand, spinning it around in her fingers. A couple of times she taps it, and her finger hovers over the glowing screen. Then she pulls it back to her chest and screws up her face.

Charlie's voice is tiny now. A thin, reedy whisper somewhere near my heart. "Will we be there in time, Marty?" he says.

"Don't worry," I say. Hen glances at me, but I think she knows who I'm talking to. "High tide's at seven, but the water'll still be in for a while after that. We'll see it. I promise."

But can I promise this? Will the dolphin be there? The ocean's not an aquarium, remember.

No. Got to be positive. Got to believe.

I want to write a poem to settle myself down, but I can't. There's only one page left in the book and I feel like it needs to be something special. Something to round everything off.

"Can I have one of them cookies now?" Charlie says, and I laugh to myself, wiping a tear from my eye.

Hen glances at me for a moment, and she looks like she's about to cry too. At first I think she must've heard Charlie as well, but then she taps her phone again and holds it to her ear, biting her thumbnail.

"Hi, Mum," she says, her voice straining. "It's me. Henrietta. I just wanted to say I . . . I'm . . . sorry, Mum."

She breaks down in tears, and I squeeze her hand. Her shoulders are shaking, and she can't speak. Then she wipes her eyes before she goes on. "I'll come home and see you tonight. No. I want . . . I'll try to stay this time. It's . . . I met someone. I'll tell you later. I can get the train. Wesley'll pick me up. Mum . . . I . . .

I love you."

She hangs up and leans her head onto my shoulder. When I glance down, I can see that her face is flooded with tears.

Arriving and Parking

I remember the outskirts of St. Bernards perfectly. How could I forget them? The RV sites and supermarkets that slowly melt into the arcades and hotels and beach shops and art galleries and pubs and cafés.

"Where d'you wanna be, then?" says the driver. It's the first thing he's said for about a half hour.

"Harbor, please," I reply, and he sucks his teeth like I've asked him to drop us on the moon. We make our way down a few steep, narrow streets, avoiding the late-season tourists who walk along the middle of the road. At one point, we take a wrong turn down a one-way. The driver swears, reverses, and pulls over outside a shop. "Harbor's two minutes down there. This is as far as I'll go."

We pay him, grab our bags, then sprint down to the harbor. It's getting much darker now. The sun is low. Its rippling reflection turns the water into liquid gold.

The memories of the town flood back to me. The smell of fish and chips. The hoards of greedy seagulls. It's like the last year never happened.

But it did of course.

I slip my backpack off and hold it to my chest. The cookie tin is hard against my ribs. Not yet. Not yet.

I press myself against the fence and scan the harbor. Nothing. I stare and bite my lip and I can't see it. *Why isn't it there?*

But then.

"What's *that*?" asks Hen, beside me.

Sure enough. A knot of people farther along are pointing out to sea, making the telltale whoops and gasps. I follow their fingers. And there it is! The dolphin! It's back! Skimming through the sparkling water, its fin slicing the gold. But *hold on* . . . there's a small shape alongside it.

"A baby as well!" whispers Charlie inside my heart. His voice is crackly. Almost silent. "A baby, Martin! Look at it."

"I've never . . . It's . . ." says Hen, but she can't finish the sentence because the dolphin is swimming toward us and Hen's totally mesmerized.

I can see a dark stripe, a scar, on the mother's tail, just above the fluke. "It's the same one!" I shout. "It's Charlie's dolphin!"

And the bag is on the floor. And the *special-leftover-from-Christmas* cookie tin is in my hands. And my fingers are under the lid. And I've lifted it off. And—

"Martin! What are you doing?!" cries a loud voice behind me.

I spin around and freeze. Mum, Dad, and a policeman are striding toward us.

Cookies

"What are you *doing*?" she repeats as she clutches me tightly, the tin hard between us.

"I . . . I . . ." I begin but before I know it we're both shaking and crying.

"I'll leave you to it," says the policeman. He tips his hat to my mum and dad then strides off. Nobody acknowledges him leaving.

"We've been so worried," sobs Mum, and the words come tumbling out breathlessly. "The alarm on your phone was going off but you weren't there and I found the paper with the train times. Then I remembered how that teacher rang up last week saying he was scared you'd do something like this." She takes a breath, then carries straight on. "So I ran to the train station and they said they'd seen you. Then the police put out a call and a policewoman traveling down south said she'd seen you acting funny. Then we called the train companies and—"

"We went straight to the airport," says Dad, his hand resting on my shoulder. "We knew where you were going, son, and there was a flight so . . . you know . . ."

And just as I'm thinking that this is the longest conversation I've had with my mum and dad in a whole year, Mum lets go of me. Her eyes flick downward. There's a moment like she's realized something she knew all along. Then, very gently, her hands slip over the sides of the *special-leftover-from-Christmas* cookie tin, and she tries to pry it out of my hands.

"No!" I say, yanking it back from her and shoving the lid back on. I'm surprised by the power of my voice. "You're not having it!"

Mum stares at me in shock.

"Come on, son," says Dad, but I struggle out from under his hand.

"*Please*, Martin," begs Mum, and I look at her, *really look at her*, for the first time in a year. Oh. She's aged. She used to have plump cheeks, but she's lost so much weight they're hollow. And her skin is pale and dull from being indoors all year. And there are rings around her eyes, and now she's crying, her weak shoulders shaking with each sob. "Please. Please."

"Jeez, Martin. Just let her have a cookie," says Hen, like I'm the cruelest person in the world. And somewhere, deep inside me, I can just about hear Charlie sadly laughing.

"They're not *cookies*!" cries Mum, turning to face Hen. "That's my son!"

The Truth

Hen's eyes look like they're about to pop out of her head.

I say nothing.

"How *could* you?" howls Mum. "How could you . . ."

Suddenly she's whacking my chest and I'm just standing there, gripping the box and taking it until the blows get lighter and lighter and she breaks down and Dad pulls her off me and holds her to him.

"You should never have done this, Martin," says Dad, over her shoulder.

And that's it.

The final straw.

I've had enough.

"I did it for you!" I shout. "I did it for the family! I did it for us!"

"Don't you shout at me," snarls Dad, finger up toward my chest.

Hen steps in front of him. "Leave him alone."

Dad looks down and seems to notice her for the first time. "What's it got to do with you?"

Hen ignores the question. "What's he done? I don't get it. Why are you screaming at him?"

Dad's body stiffens.

There's a tense silence. I take a deep breath. And then I tell her. Slowly and softly. "I stole Charlie's ashes. From the jar . . . the *urn* on the mantel. I put them in the cookie tin. And I ran away."

"How could you?" sobs Mum again.

"You don't get it, do you?" I cry. "Charlie's dead. *Dead.*"

"Stop it!" cries Mum, burying her head in Dad's chest.

But I won't stop. Not now. "He wouldn't want to sit there on the mantel in a stupid urn. He'd want to be . . ."

I cast my arm across the harbor. Behind me, the sun is sinking lower. The dolphin is still there, splashing around just feet away from us. The tourists are still pointing at it and cooing like we don't exist.

"No!" says Mum. "No. He needs to be with us. With his family."

"But he'll always be with us," I said. "We'll never forget him, will we? How could we? He's in all of us, all the time. But we've got to say goodbye."

"No!" says Mum, and her hands are on the tin again but now her grip is weaker.

"He'd want us to live, Mum," I say. "He'd want us to be alive like the dolphin."

A few moments pass. Then Dad looks at me and his face folds into a frown. "Hang on," he says. "The alarm going off on your phone to wake us up. The train times right next to it. The way you left the lid off your brother's urn so we'd see what you'd done. The tin gone, but the tray of cookies left behind. . . ." He pauses. "You wanted us to follow you, didn't you?"

The question stops me like a hand in the chest. I open my mouth and my lips try to form an answer, but the truth is that I really don't know. Maybe I did. Maybe I wasn't running away from Mum and Dad at all. Maybe I was running toward them.

Dad gently places his hand on my shoulder, and Mum tilts her head to one side and looks at me, a bit like how Charlie used to do.

I feel my eyes drawn to the water. And for the first time, Mum and Dad seem to notice the dolphin. It's right by the harbor wall, playing with its baby. They're flipping and twisting and corkscrewing over each other.

I've no idea how long we're standing there. Time doesn't seem important to me anymore. But, ever so slowly, Mum's fingers slip off the tin and she turns to me. There's a terrible moment when I think she's going to scream again, but then she just leans forward and kisses the tin and whispers goodbye; then she nods her head and puts her hand over her mouth. I realize that everything has changed.

"Do it quick," she whispers, her eyes screwed up and her shoulders shaking. "Do it quick, Marty."

"Go on, son," says Dad grimly, and he pats me on the arm. "For Charlie."

I turn to Hen. She's wiping her eyes. Her makeup

has run down her cheeks, and she smiles at me through her tears.

And Charlie's there again, right there, in front of me, in my heart, and all around me. And his voice is as strong as ever. "Can I swim with the dolphin now, Martin?" he grins. "Can I?"

I rip the lid off the tin, and I stare at the gray powder inside that used to be my brother. Then, without looking at anyone else, I turn and tip it out over the railings. And a gust of wind catches Charlie's ashes and swirls them out over the water in a beautiful silver cloud.

Then something incredible happens. Or maybe it doesn't happen. Maybe I imagine it. But it doesn't matter because, for one beautiful moment, what I imagine and what's real are one and the same thing.

With an enormous splash of spray that catches the light, the baby dolphin leaps out of the water and into the sky, right through Charlie's cloud. It hangs in the air for a moment, whipping the ashes into dancing whirls that mingle with the golden drops of water, before it plummets down and disappears into the dark sea. A spray of tiny droplets scatter down onto the water afterward, churning and rippling on the surface.

And now I know what my final poem will be.

Leaping Dolphin, Part 2

Your life is a leaping dolphin.
A brief moment of
Exquisite beauty and possibility
Before you return to blankness.
Blackness.
But after you land
And disappear,
Those tiny golden droplets of water
That each carry your reflection
Shower down,
Creating endless ripples
That spread out forever,
Colliding endlessly
And mingling together to form
A permanent reminder of who you are.
Charlie.
My brother.

By Martin Tompkins
Age 13